Knight and Alize

REVENGE IN THE STREETS

MZ. KB

Knight and Alize

Copyright 2022 by Mz. KB

Published by Grand Penz Publications

The future looked bright for fourteen-year-old Alizé Washington. However, after being forced to watch her father's murder, life for her changes dramatically, and the turn of events is set to change her entire outlook on the world forever. Learning that her mother had been lying, and that she was the cause of all her problems, Alizé didn't know who to turn to for help.

With guilt consuming her every waking hour, Serena Washington has a complete mental breakdown, leaving her two daughters alone to fend for themselves. When Serena is admitted into the psych ward, she is too scared to tell them about her children.

Realizing her mom isn't coming home any time soon, Alizé accepts that she and her sister are alone in this cold world, and it is down to her to make sure they survive. Trying to keep them both together, she decides they must leave their home and start over somewhere new. Alizé must do whatever to keep herself and her little sister safe. While trying to keep everything together, Alizé is forced to make enough money to keep them alive by any means necessary, even if that means losing herself in the process.

With the help of someone she thought was her friend and the generosity of a stranger, Alizé finally starts to rebuild her life, but not everything is as wonderful as it first appears. After being forced to sleep with men for money and at the hands of the man who is forcing her to do the things she doesn't want to do, Alizé reaches the lowest point of her life. While considering ending it all, she meets Knight Carter. Is he her savior and the one who will make her trust in love again? Or is he just another man who will hurt her heart?

Hell-bent on avenging her daddy's death, Alizé has the toughest decision of her life when she must choose between love and the revenge her heart so desperately seeks.

When Ava meets Alizé, they form an unlikely duo with one thing in mind: to kill the man they blame for ruining their lives. The bond they have is like no other, and both women prove to be just the friend that the other one needs.

Knight never thought he would want to settle down with one woman, but meeting Alizé changes everything for the young boss. Will he convince his love to stay with him when she realizes who he is?

CHAPTER 1

Alizé Washington

I was sitting in my room scrolling through Facebook when I heard my mama calling me from downstairs. "Alizé, will you come down here and help me get this table ready for dinner, please?"

I put down my phone and made my way to the kitchen. Dinner time was always a big thing in our family, and no matter what you were doing or where you were, you had to have your ass here by seven o'clock on the dot so we could all eat together. That was mama's rule, and she wouldn't change it for shit.

I took the knives and forks from the kitchen and started setting them on the table for the four of us to eat dinner. I heard my daddy's car pulling up in the driveway. Looking up, it was five minutes to seven, and as always, he arrived right on time. Two minutes later, I heard the front door close. My younger sister's footsteps could be heard clicking on the marble floor, where she was running through the foyer in her shoes to greet him as she always did when he came home from work. Both of us were daddy's girls, but being that my sister is the youngest, she is very much daddy's baby.

My dad didn't have a job like most parents. He didn't go to work in an office or a store or even drive a truck. He was a hustler, and no one could change a single thing about Meek Washington. Lord knows my mama tried enough over the years. My parents didn't think I knew what he did when he was at work, but I had found out a long time ago that he wasn't like most fathers, and we weren't like most families.

When I was eight years old, I remember a girl at school telling me she couldn't come to my birthday party because my daddy was a drug dealer and a murderer. She's told my entire class that her mother said he was an evil man who should be locked up. I was mad as hell. I was a daddy's girl through and through, so I waited for her during recess and punched her in her throat. My parents got called into the school to see the principal to discuss my fighting. I never told them the real reason I hit that girl. They just thought it was kids being kids, and that's how everyone dealt with shit in the hood. My daddy told me he was proud of me for not getting my ass beat. Although we are now fourteen, the bitch has never said a word to me again, and I never revealed the truth about the fight. As far as my parents were concerned, I still thought my dad was a real estate agent, and I played along with it all day to keep the peace.

My mama put dishes of jerk chicken, rice, potato salad, and coleslaw on the table, and we all sat around to eat. Mama served the food, and as we do every night, we took turns to tell each other about our day.

"How has everyone's day been today?" my dad asked as he heaped food onto his fork.

"School was good today, daddy. A dance is coming up, and I need something to wear, pleaaaseee!" my eleven-year-old sister Affinity said while grinning at my daddy.

We all laughed at her. For her to only be eleven, she was such a little diva already.

"Of course, princess. Your mama can take you both shopping this weekend, and how about you, ZéZé? How was the exam?" he asked, calling me by the pet name he gave me when I was a baby.

"I had a good day too, daddy. I got an A on my math exam, and I got the singing part that I was telling you about in the school show," I told him.

"You're so clever, baby girl. I knew you would do it, and you have the voice of an angel so I never doubted that you would get the part. And how was your day dear?" he asked my mom.

Before she got the chance to answer him, there was a banging at the door. My dad instructed us to all stay where we were while he went to see what the noise was all about, but we followed him anyway. As he opened the front door, he was hit with the handle of a gun and knocked to the floor. Three masked men came into the dining room with guns drawn, pointing them at us and screaming for us to stay still. Another man with a mask came in behind them, dragging my daddy's unconscious body on the floor behind him like he was a rag doll.

The first man grabbed hold of my mom and forced her to sit on the couch. He shouted at me and Affinity to sit next to her and not to move. We quickly obeyed the order and ran to my mother's side. Two of the men pulled my daddy up and put him in the chair he had been sitting in moments before. One of the men pulled out a rope from his pocket and started tying my daddy to the chair. My sister was screaming, and my mama tried to calm her down and shield her eyes from what was happening. She pulled me closer to her while the men were hitting my daddy, trying to bring him to.

One of the men went outside and came back in with another man. Unlike the others, this man wasn't wearing a mask. He was in a cream color suit and a long trench coat with really expensive-looking shiny shoes on. He looked at my mom and winked his eye at her.

"Hello darling, did you miss me?" he quizzed as he bent down and kissed my mother's lips. I couldn't believe she actually kissed this man back even though my dad was sitting there tied up and getting beat on.

"What are you doing here, Chief?" she said, eyes wide with anticipation of what he was going to say.

I had never met Chief, but I'd overheard plenty about him. He was the connect. I knew that much. I also know that he and my father used to be friends, but they had stopped fucking with each other just after I was born. I used to listen to my mom and my aunties talking. When these bitches were sipping that Henny, they were sure to spit all kinds of shit that they shouldn't be repeating.

"I came to discuss some business with your husband, my love. Apparently, yours is not the only pussy we've been sharing. Isn't that right, Meek?" he said, looking at my father.

Walking toward him, he delivered a left hook to his head, quickly followed by an uppercut from the right. Now that he was alert again, my father looked at the man he once considered a friend and spat blood from his mouth, which landed on the man's shiny, expensive-looking shoe.

"I have eyes everywhere, Meek. What makes you think you could fuck my wife and I wouldn't find out? You know who I am, and you know I won't tolerate the disrespect you have shown me."

"Fuck you, Chief. I did that shit the exact way you did, my nigga! Do you think I don't know that you have been fucking Serena for years? Why the fuck do you think Ava came to me in the first place? You were too busy fucking my wife to see that your own wife needed you. It was me who comforted her and kept her warm at night. It was me who she fell in love with, me who she thought about when she had to take your little dick, and it was my name she was screaming when she cum! You see, while you were fucking that whore over there, you pushed Ava and me together. We're leaving you both and taking our children with us," my daddy revealed while spitting even more blood from his mouth onto the man's shoe.

"You think Ava loves you? Don't make me laugh, my friend. That bitch loves only herself and her precious fucking kids. She has no capacity to love. She is driven purely by power. Money is the only way to make that sour old bitch cum! You will never see my wife again. Ya' heard?"

"She loves me more than she ever loved you. She despises you. You have no power. You are a pathetic excuse for a man. You come into my house and tie me up in front of my children 'cuz you couldn't come and fight me like a real man. You get some little bitch niggas in masks to come in here first because you are weak. You've always been weak.

A real man would've dealt with this shit in the streets. You're nothing but a coward nigga. Babies, remember daddy loves you both. Serena, get your hoe ass up and take my children out of the room now so this bitch can do what he came to do. On my dead mother, you know I would kick your ass if it were just you and me, you pussy ass motherfucker. Just know one thing. I'll be waiting for you in hell, my nigga!" my dad gritted.

Just as my mom stood to take us out of the room, one of the men grabbed her and forced her to sit down. He grabbed both my mom and me by the hair, and we were made to watch as the man in the suit pulled a sword out of his waist. He raised his hands above his shoulders like it was a baseball bat and brought it down with such force that it cut my daddy's head off his shoulders in one swift movement.

All that could be heard was my mom and I screaming, which had my sister crying and trying to get out of my mom's grip to see what was happening. I watched my dad's head roll onto the carpet. I sat stunned, not knowing what to say or what to do. All I knew was that my daddy was dead, and my life would never be the same.

My mom quickly shut up when a masked man pointed his gun at her, but she shocked the shit out of me with her next move. She stood up, walked over to my daddy's killer, and kissed him hard.

"Now we can be together, darling," she professed quietly, thinking I couldn't hear her.

"Don't be fucking stupid, Serena. I would never leave my wife and kids for you. You always knew what this was, ma, so don't trip now. Plus, I need a rider by my side, and after watching how you just did your husband, I can't trust you. Keep it wet, baby. I'll slide by and see you soon," he said while slapping my mom's ass.

"You bastard! What am I supposed to do now, Chief? I thought we were going to be together?" she was screaming now and trying to hit him in his chest.

"Help her clean this shit up, and y'all can go home. I'm going to go home and give my wife her gift," he stated with a chuckle as he picked up my daddy's severed head by his hair, placed it into a duffle bag, and left with it, completely dismissing my mom's question.

As I sat there stunned, watching the men help my mom clean up the blood and remove what was left of my daddy's body, I vowed that one day, no matter what it took, I would make that nigga pay for what he just did, and so would this bitch who called herself being a wife and mother. She proved with her actions that she is a snake ass whore, and I would never forgive her for this as long as I live. On my dead daddy, they would pay for what happened here tonight, one way or another. I vowed to avenge my dad's murder no matter what it took.

CHAPTER 2

Serena Washington

I couldn't believe my eyes when Chief walked in here tonight. This nigga had me believing that we would be together once I left Meek and he left Ava. I felt like such a fool to have trusted this man, and now I was stuck with no one and nothing. Things haven't been right with Meek and me for a while, but if I'm honest, I was fucking Chief way before the problems in my marriage showed up. I didn't realize my husband knew about our affair, and I damn sure didn't know he was fucking that bitch, Ava. She always got what I fucking wanted, and it wasn't fair. Ever since we were young, everyone has always been all about Ava. Now, because of her, I have lost my husband and my man. I swear, one day, I'm going to kill that bitch.

Back in the day, before we all had children, the four of us were firm friends. As our men's positions in the streets grew, so did their animosity toward each other. Chief had this raw ambition that Meek just didn't possess. That's one thing that attracted me to him. While Meek was content with running the city, Chief had dreams of running the whole damn country. Eventually, Chief started making moves that Meek just wasn't fucking with, and the crew was divided, with most of their friends choosing to stay and roll with Meek. In the end, it came between them, and the problems escalated into a full-on gang war over money and turf. Without a doubt, the rivalry between our husbands ended my friendship with Ava. We both chose to stand by our men, and rightly so.

I heard through the grapevine that she had given birth to a son not long after we stopped speaking. After Alizé was born, I didn't go out as much as I used to and lost contact with many old friends. I wasn't moving in those circles anymore, so I never heard anything about Ava again for a long time.

It was just coming up to Alizé's first birthday, and I was organizing her birthday party. I was out shopping, struggling with all my bags and Alizé in her stroller when my phone rang. I went to answer the call and dropped my damn car keys down the drains and into the sewer. I was beyond angry right now. Meek was away dealing with some business again, so I couldn't even get him to bring my spare key from the house. This meant I would have to get a taxi to take me home to get the key and bring me back.

I dropped my bags in frustration as Alizé started crying, and I just wanted to cry with her.

"Serena?" I heard.

As I looked up, I was staring at Chief, and he was looking like a boss. I could tell he had leveled up in the game since we were last in each other's company just by the clothes he was wearing and the ice on his grill.

"Oh, hi, Chief," I spoke, trying to keep my composure and stop my body from betraying me. This nigga was fine, and he had my panties wet as hell.

"What's wrong, ma? You look like you want to scream. Who's this little cutie?" he asked, looking at my baby girl in her stroller. She had now found her pacifier and was sucking on it as if her life depended on it.

"I just dropped my damn keys in the drain. Meek is away, and I need to get home to get my spare key. I left my daughter's diaper bag in the car with her bottle in it, as we were only collecting some items from the store. It's almost time for her bottle, so I need to get going. It was nice to see you. Take care of yourself," I relayed, trying to walk around him.

"Let me help you. I can drive you home. My car is just over the road. You can get your key, feed this pretty lady, and then I'll bring you back here to get your car."

"Erm, it's fine. I can just get a taxi. It's no trouble. Thank you, though," I replied, knowing that Meek would want to kill me if he knew I was talking to Chief, let alone contemplating letting him drive me to the house where we laid our heads.

"I insist. Come on, just because I have my differences with Meek, does that mean you can't speak to me? We're old friends, Serena. Come on, let me help you," he urged while picking up my bags.

I wanted to protest, but it started to rain, and it was pouring down within seconds. I couldn't keep my daughter out here any longer, especially not over a beef that wasn't even mine. It's not like Chief would hurt us. We went back too far for that. So, I followed him to his car and directed him to our new home.

* * *

Once we got there, I said I would only be a minute and come straight back out. I got inside, found Alizé her bottle, and set her down on the couch while I went in search of my spare key. When I came back into the room, Chief was sitting on the couch with Alizé on his shoulder, burping her.

Soon she fell asleep in his arms. He lay her down on the seat and moved closer to me.

"I found my spare key. Would you mind taking me back to the car now?" I asked.

"What's the rush? Let's have a drink for old time's sake. You look like you could do with it. You said Meek was away, and the little lady is sleeping now, so it would be a shame to disturb her. I'll get one of my men to get your car."

"Ok, I suppose one drink won't hurt. Let me put the baby in her crib," I told him as I handed him the spare key to give to the guy who he was sending for my car.

When I came back downstairs fifteen minutes later, after washing, changing, and putting the baby back to sleep, Chief was sitting on the back patio smoking a blunt and drinking Patrón from a glass. When he noticed me, he beckoned for me to join him. I went and sat down next to him, and he handed me a glass. I drank a sip and winced as it burned the back of my throat. I took a pull from the blunt that he handed me and instantly felt my body relax. Easing back into the chair, it occurred to me that I hadn't realized how much I had needed to relax for once. Since Alizé had been born, I felt like I hadn't stopped and taken ten minutes for myself. Meek was always working, so most of the childcare and household chores were my responsibility, and I suddenly felt like I needed a break. Some time to just be Serena, so I downed the rest of the drink and finished the blunt.

One drink led to two, then three. It wasn't long before the whole bottle was gone, and I was drunk as hell. One thing led to another, and we ended up fucking right there in my back garden. It was the most exciting sex of my life, and I had never felt so alive. Chief was like a drug to me, and I couldn't get enough of him. He was like my own personal brand of heroin, and I was a fiend who was hooked from the first hit. Our affair has continued on and off for the last thirteen years. I know I was stupid to be risking my marriage and comfortable lifestyle for sex, but the urge was uncontrollable. Chief possessed a mad power over me, and I couldn't walk away from him if I'd tried. My body yearned for him, as did my need for the excitement our affair gave me. When I found out I was pregnant just over a year later with Affinity, I could've died. To this day, I still don't know whether Meek or Chief is her biological father. I always swore I would take that shit to my grave and not let them ever find out, but Chief wasn't stupid. He told me she looked like his oldest son and his baby daughter. He made it known that as far as anyone need know, she was Meek's child, and that was that.

It's only in the last year or two that we have talked about being together properly. Now that the children are all older, it would be easier to explain. Both of us were in loveless marriages and craved the love we felt for each other. To hear him say those things to me tonight broke my heart into a million pieces. Well, what was left of my heart after seeing my husband's head getting chopped off and finding out he had been cheating on me for all these years. I felt so betrayed, but who was I kidding? He only did to me what I had been doing to him. Seeing Chief so angry let me know I had been a fool to believe him. He clearly still loved his wife, and he never intended to leave that bougie ass bitch for me. Now my kids and I were here without shit all 'cuz I wanted to have a sneaky ass pussy and fuck outside of my marriage. My husband's death would forever haunt me, as would the look on his face when he called me a whore.

I finally settled both of my children down and continued trying to clean up the mess created in my home by Chief and his fuckeries. I didn't even know where he hid the money or anything. I had fucked up royally this time, and I had no idea what the fuck I was going to do. I needed a plan on how I would survive now that my husband was dead.

* * *

The next few months were a blur. I couldn't tell anyone that my husband was dead, so I had to tell people he was away on business. Then, as time went on, I had to tell people that Meek had left me. It was better than the truth. How could I tell anyone that my side nigga found out my husband was fucking his wife and killed him? Chief was a fucking hypocrite. I hadn't seen or heard from him since the night he killed Meek. He'd had one of his men slide through with some money two or three times, but whenever I asked about him, they just told me to move on. Chief had fucked my life up and gone home to his family like everything was sweet, while I was left trying to hold it all together with two kids who looked at me with such disgust in their eyes in burned my soul.

I was so depressed that I had gotten my doctor to prescribe me something to help me. The Prozac he had given me had long ago stopped working, so I started to self-medicate. First, with just weed, but I dabbed in coke and heroin every so often. That every so often turned into every damn day, and I had sold everything of any value. I had nothing left to give, and there was no way I could get a job looking as rough as what I did. I begged Chief for help, but the bastard changed his phone number and went ghost on my ass.

The last straw came one day in the store when I didn't even have enough money to get food to make the kids for their dinner. I fumbled around in my purse for some change but still came up short. It was the most embarrassing moment of my life. I went outside the store and dropped to the floor, shaking and crying uncontrollably. It was like it sent me over the edge, and I had a mental breakdown right there in the middle of the street. All the feelings I had suppressed for months had finally come to a head, and I blew a gasket. I sat there on the floor, crying for what seemed like an eternity. People were trying to talk to me, but I was in another world.

The next thing I knew I was in a hospital room, handcuffed to a bed and high as fuck. I didn't know what they had given my ass, but I was flying. I just knew that if I told them my name, they would find out about my kids and then take them away from me. So, I gave them a fake name, and I just had to ride it out for a week or two, and they would let me go home. Alizé was fourteen. She was old enough to look after her sister for a little while. They'll be fine, and I can spend the time recuperating. The doctors had already told me I'd had some sort of breakdown, which was stress related. If only they fucking knew... watching your side nigga kill your fucking husband will really fuck with a chick's mind.

CHAPTER 3

Alizé

"But I want mommy! You're not the boss of me, Alizé!" Affinity screamed at the top of her lungs.

She was really starting to make me mad. I don't know where the hell my mother has got to. She is usually here when we get home from school, but when we came home on Monday, she wasn't here, and I haven't seen or heard from her since. I kept telling my sister that she wouldn't be long, but it's now Thursday, and I still haven't heard anything.

Things have been real bad at home since my daddy was killed, but you would think my mom would try to make shit ok. Instead, she sits around all damn day, popping pills and injecting that devil drug into her arm. I miss the days that I used to come home to a clean house, with something always cooking and two parents who loved us. There was hardly any food in the house, but I managed to cook dinner for us both. Now Affinity wouldn't go to bed until mom got here. I tried phoning her the first night but soon learned her phone was at home when it started ringing in the other room. Lord knows where she has got to, but I can't keep worrying about her grown ass. I needed to look after myself and my sister. I was all she had right now. Had my mother not been whoring her pussy around the way she was, my dad would still be here, and we wouldn't be living the hell that we're living right now. I'll never forgive Serena for her actions, and as soon as I was old enough, I was planning to leave home and never look back.

I needed to figure out a way to get some money and fast, or we wouldn't be eating this weekend. I searched high and low and looked in every closet, drawer, and cabinet in the entire house, but I only came up with forty-two dollars and some change. That would get a little food to last us a day or two. Hopefully, by then, my mom would show her face.

"Alizé, I'm scared. Daddy's gone, and now mommy is gone too. It's just you and me, but you're not old enough to look after us. Will we have to live with strangers?" Affinity cried from the doorway of my room.

I patted the bed next to me, she came to sit down, and I hugged her tight.

"I'll never leave you, sissy. You have to keep this our secret. It's the only way those people won't come and take us. If anyone finds out that Serena isn't here, they will be on our asses, and we can't take that chance. They won't let us be together, so promise me you will keep this quiet. I'm going to think of a way to get money. We're going to be ok. I promise."

"I've got money! I have my piggy bank. I have at least a hundred dollars in there. One day I saw daddy hiding some money in the floor, but he told me not to tell mommy cuz she would spend it all on make-up and shoes. He gave me money and told me it was our secret. Lemme show you."

My sister led me into my daddy's closet, lifted the rug, and pulled up a loose board. She stuffed her hand down into the hole and came out with a wad of money. I was so damn happy! There were at least a thousand dollars in there. At least we would be able to survive now. I would use the money to keep the lights on, do some grocery shopping, and pay for Affinity to have lunch at school. At least we would have all the things we really needed until my mother showed her face again, whenever the fuck that may be.

"Sissy, you saved us. This is enough money for us to survive until mommy comes home. Tomorrow morning before school, I will take you to get breakfast at the diner. After school, we will get some groceries to last us the weekend. She can't be much longer now."

Eight Months Later

"Affinity, will you please just get your bag, and let's get out of here? If they come back, they are going to take us away. Please, I need you to just listen to me."

"Where are we going? I don't want to leave. I'll miss my friends," she whined.

"We are going to Chicago. Remember my friend Yanni? She is going to help us. Come on. We don't have time for this."

I had packed as much as I could into two big duffle bags and got us bus tickets. My next-door neighbor told me that CPS came over there asking her mom questions about us. I knew we had to leave, or they would take my sister away from me. Don't get me wrong, I had often thought that she would be better off with a real family, in a real home, not having to live the way we have been, but I can't bear the thought of losing her. She is all I have left in this world.

It's been over eight months, and there is still no sign of Serena. I stopped calling her my mom when she abandoned us and left a fourteen-year-old as the sole caregiver to an eleven-year-old. My childhood was over, and I had been doing all kinds of shit to keep us alive. I started off stealing food just to keep us fed. About three months back, I met Yanni. She used to run drugs with the boys from the block. I met her one day in the store. I had been in there trying to boost something to eat when the store owner caught me. He grabbed hold of me and pulled me to the front of the store. While still holding on to me, he picked up the phone to call the police. By then, I was crying, petrified that the police would come and find out that my mom had left us. I knew they would try to take Affinity away from me.

"Come on now, boss. I'll pay for what she took, and she won't come back here. Ain't that right?" I turned to see a girl that I didn't know holding out a twenty-dollar bill to the man.

"I promise I won't come back. I'm sorry. Please don't call the police." I pleaded.

When we got outside the store, the girl told me to follow her.

"Aye, I'm Yanni. I've seen you around a few times. What's your deal? Why do I always see you trying to steal from these whack ass shops?"

"I'm Alizé," I stated shyly. "I do it 'cuz it's the only way my sister and I eat some nights. I don't have a choice."

"What about your parents? They fiends?"

"Something like that. Anyway, thank you for helping me. I need to get this back to my sister."

"Wait, come back. I might know a way you can earn some money. You know how to keep your mouth shut, though, right?"

"Yea, of course. I'm desperate."

"Meet me back here tomorrow at four o'clock. I'll show you what to do. Here, hold this," Yanni said, handing me fifty dollars.

"Thank you. I will. I promise."

I walked home happy as hell. I ordered us a pizza as a treat for my sister. I didn't know what I would have to do for the money, but I didn't care. At that stage, I would've done anything.

* * *

The next day, I went back to the store and met Yanni at four o'clock, just like she said. She introduced me to her crew. She always hung with the boys. She said it was better protection out here. They had me running rocks to fiends all evening that first night. Then she gave me some to hold, and they told me where to take it, and I did. I would get a percentage of each deal I did. Within the first week, I had earned enough money to get the light bill paid and do grocery shopping. Within the first month, I got Affinity new clothes, did the shopping, and we still had money left over. Things were finally starting to look up for me. I knew I was taking a risk, but it's the only way I knew that my sister and I would survive.

Then last week, Yanni almost got caught on her way back from doing a pickup. She had four pounds of crack. She had to run from the police and drop some of it. The boss was a guy called Man-Man. He was mad crazy at her when she told him what had happened. He beat her ass badly, and she ran away to Chicago to link up with one of her friends so she could try to pay him off. She said he has a big house, and we can all stay there. He would expect us to run for him the same as what he had been doing here but on a bigger scale. More risk meant more reward, and what the fuck did I have to stick around here for?

As soon as I found out that the CPS motherfuckers were coming by, I knew I had to get my sister out of this mess and move on. We could have a fresh start, and Yanni's friend agreed to sign the forms to get Affinity back in school there, too. So far, I had managed to keep her in school and keep her ass fed and clothed. If my mother came back, then that was on her. She never should've fucking left us to start with. I will never understand what her problem is or how someone can be so selfish to leave a fourteen-year-old taking care of her eleven-year-old sister for such a long period of time.

I grabbed my sister and our bags, leaving our old life behind us. I stopped on the corner and glanced back at the home that'd been the setting for so many memories. Not all of them were good, but they weren't all bad either. I knew I would never return to this house again. I said a silent prayer to my daddy, asking him to guide us and look after us on this next step. He would be absolutely heartbroken to see what had become of us, but I know he would be proud of me for holding shit down for my sister. But shit, what other damn choice did I have?

CHAPTER 4

Yanni Samaras

I lied to everyone about why I had left and started over in Chicago. I did lose some of the weight that I picked up, and Man-Man was hella pissed with me, but I didn't run away. He sent me here to 'look after' his brother. Not only did Man-Man and his brother run drugs all over the damn country, but they also ran girls, too. Being sent here was my punishment for fucking up, but I've got used to being treated like an object, something to pass around. Long ago, I learned to suppress my feelings about anything, so I literally have no emotions left inside me. I buried that shit so deep down that I doubt they will ever be found again. Being void of emotion is the only way I've made it through the last few years. I have been working for them since I was thirteen. I ran away from home because I was getting raped by my mom's boyfriend at every given opportunity, and when I told her about it, she beat my ass and accused me of trying to take her man. I stole four hundred dollars from them while they were asleep before setting light to the house with them inside. I walked away and never looked back. I didn't even stay long enough to see if they'd made it out alive.

Everything was good for a while, but it didn't take long 'til

I ran out of money and started stealing just to feed myself. The day I met Alizé wasn't a coincidence. It was just how Man-Man patterned it. They got me the same way I got Alizé. I met a girl in the store who offered to help me, and I let her. That proved to be the biggest mistake of my life so far. What I didn't know back then was that I wasn't special. They didn't want to help me. They picked girls who looked alone, poor, or vulnerable, and they targeted them.

Within months, I had gone from running drugs around to being forced into having sex with older men for money. Man-Man took seventy percent of what we earned and told us it was because he looked after us. He called us all 'his special girls.' The day I met Alizé, it was because he had spotted her stealing from the store a few days before. He knew his grown ass couldn't approach her, so when he saw her again, he sent me into the store after her. The store owner was his friend, and he was in on the whole charade. He would act like he was furious and threaten to phone the police. That's how he made sure that the girls complied... by giving them no other option. Man-Man would let his nasty ass fuck the girls when he was breaking them in, so it was a win-win for them both.

I used to feel bad about being the one who lured them in, but shit, it was a dog-eat-dog world. It was them or me, and I chose myself every single time. Not only that, but Man-Man was not the kind of person you said no to. I had to learn that the hard way. The only thing I felt bad about this time was that I actually liked her. Alizé wasn't like most of the girls I met. She was intelligent and funny. She wasn't getting high or out here fucking and causing problems. She was a good girl who was dealt a bad hand. You could tell she was green as hell just by listening to some of the shit she said, but she was learning quickly. I felt bad for her after hearing what happened with her parents. Shit, her mom sounded like she could compete against my own in the world's worst mother competition.

When she told me about the CPS turning up and asking the neighbors questions about her and her sister, I knew I could get her to come here to link me. I had brought four girls here with me, and Hardcore had taken them to be broken in. I was just happy as fuck that I didn't have to fuck as much as the others. I was trying to work my way up to where I could just manage the girls and not have to do any of that other shit anymore. It's not like there was a way out for a chick like me. This is my life now, so I just had to make the most of what I had. I'm just grateful to have a roof over my head and clothes on my back.

"Hey, daddy, she fell for it. Alizé is convinced that CPS was there to take her sister away and split them up. She phoned me, sounding like she was scared, so I told her I could help her. She and her sister are on the way to the bus station as we speak," I relayed to Man-Man when he answered the phone.

"I knew it would work. Good girl, you made daddy proud. Get back to work now and earn off some of that dough you fucked up on. I'ma slide through in a few days," he replied as he put the phone down.

He loved it when we called him daddy, and if it kept a smile on his ugly face, then it's whatever. All I cared about was him not beating my ass for the work I lost. The last time he beat me, I couldn't get out of bed for days. I was beyond fucked up. He broke my ribs and blacked both my eyes.

When I got back in the house, Man-Man's brother Hardcore was there. This nigga would be fine as hell if it weren't for his bad ass attitude and penchant for teenage girls. Standing at over six feet tall, he towered over me. His caramel skin was blemish free, apart from a scar on his left cheek, but that just added to his sex appeal. His eyes were a deep shade of brown and slightly slanted. The tattoos which adorned both of his arms were sticking out of the short sleeves on his Gucci tee.

"Where the fuck have you been?" he spat as soon as I walked in.

"I was just on the phone with your brother, and I went for a walk to see if I could spot any new potential," I lied.

"Where is this bitch you were talkin' 'bout?"

"She's on the way. She will be here by morning. Don't scare her, though. Let me ease her in."

"Bitch, who you telling what to fucking do? I'm not my brother. you better get to know who the fuck is in charge around here."

And just like that, I knew this nigga was gone be a problem. His bi-polar ass attitude was already getting old. I couldn't keep up with his moods. They switched so fast that a bitch was getting whiplash just trying.

* * *

The next day, I went to pick Alizé up from the bus station. Hardcore let me use his car, which I was happy about. It was much easier than the three buses it would've taken me to get there without it. Her little sister was cute, but she had one hell of a mouth on her. I would have to tame that shit quickly before she got herself in trouble. I just know that Hardcore will put her ass on the track if her mouth gets too smart, or she gets too rude to him. As long as Alizé stays in her lane, I think we will be able to keep her sister out of it, at least for the time being.

When we got back to the house, this nigga was like a different fucking person altogether. I told you about his fucking bi-polar attitude. One minute, he was an asshole, the next, he was actually quite likable if you could look past the fact that he was a plain psycho.

"Hey, you must be Alizé and Affinity. Yanni has told me so much about you both. She will show you to your bedrooms. Once you're both settled in, I was thinking I would take you all for some food somewhere."

"Ok, thank you so much for having us here. It means a lot to us. I promise we won't be any trouble at all," Alizé said sweetly.

I took them both upstairs to show them their rooms. They were both excited and happy. It was good to see Alizé really showing her age when she saw the beautiful room Hardcore had set out for her. It had its own bathroom and walk-in closet. There was a door that led directly into Affinity's room, which also had its own closet and bathroom.

"Yesterday, after you said you were coming, I went out shopping to get you both a few things. Hardcore gave me some money to hook you both up. I know you had to leave most of your shit behind. Everything the both of you could need is in the bags on your beds. And you know your girl chose you both some real fire shit too," I informed them.

Affinity ran straight into her room to start looking through her stuff.

"Thanks, Yanni. You don't know how much you saved me. I will forever thank God for the day I met you. You came into my life when I needed someone. You have gone above and beyond for me when you didn't have to, so thank you! You're the best friend ever," Alizé said as she hugged me.

Leaving them both in their bedrooms to look through their stuff, I went back downstairs feeling guilty. For the first time since this all started, I actually liked this chick. If we had met under different circumstances, we could've really been friends. Usually, I didn't get close to the new recruits. The guilt would consume me if I did. Alizé was different. I genuinely like her, but it's every man, or woman in this case, for themselves.

Hardcore was downstairs in his man cave smoking on a blunt. This motherfucker was really sitting in there stroking his dick while watching the camera he had set up in Alizé's room. I didn't even know this fucker had done that. It made me ask myself where he had cameras in this damn place. I made a note to myself to thoroughly inspect my bedroom before I go to bed tonight.

"Come over here, Yanni," he instructed, patting the chair next to him while still stroking his hand up and down his hard dick.

I made my way to sit down next to him, but he pulled me onto his lap.

"Come show me how you ride this big motherfucker, come, and make your ass clap for daddy. Do it just the way I like," he said as he started pulling at my jeans.

I stood back up, pulled my top over my head, and threw it down next to me. I slowly eased out of my skin-tight jeans. I stood there in nothing but my bra and panties. I learned a long time ago that saying no and acting shy would only get my ass beat, so I faked a smile and obliged. I pulled my panties down and licked my fingers. I transferred some of the wetness to my pussy, seeing as it was as dry as the desert at the thought of fucking this man, but at least he wasn't ugly like his brother. Then I lowered myself down onto his big dick and rode like my life depended on it. Technically I did. I know I had to keep Hardcore happy, or he would send me back to Man-Man. He was the lesser of two evils, and I already knew I was better off here.

Pulling my nipples free, he sucked on each one while guiding me up and down on his big pole. His eyes were on the screen the whole time, watching Alizé as she tried on different outfits. Within minutes, he tensed up and grunted as he emptied his load into me. As soon as he let me go, I got up and went into the bathroom he had installed in the basement and got a warm cloth so I could wash his dick off. Once I was satisfied that he was clean, I pulled my clothes on and left to go to my room to shower and change.

"Y'all got an hour, and I'll take y'all out to eat. Seeing as you've been so good, I'll let you choose where we go," he said with a smirk on his face. At least with this one, he was happy some of the time. Man-Man was a pure asshole twenty-four hours a day.

I made my way to my bedroom. I stopped and knocked on Alizé's door.

"Come in." she sang from inside.

"Hey, we're going out to eat in an hour. Be ready, and I'll meet you downstairs. I'm just going to shower and change. Hardcore is a boss in these parts, so make sure you look cute 'cuz he likes everything to be perfect. In his eyes, we are all a reflection of him, so it's imperative that we look the part at all times," I advised.

"Well, that will be easy with these cute clothes y'all got me. I'll tell Affinity to get herself ready and we'll meet you downstairs. Thank you again, Yanni. I can't wait to start working so I can repay you for everything you've done for us," she replied happily.

CHAPTER 5

Alizé

I was so happy that Yanni invited us here. The house was dope, and the guy seemed nice enough too. When I saw the mountain of clothes, accessories, and shoes that Yanni had got for me, I was hyped. I haven't seen Affinity this happy since my dad was alive.

Inside the bags, we had both gotten new iPhones, and Affinity even had a laptop to help her with her schoolwork. I couldn't wait to get her enrolled in school again. She needed to make some new friends. Even though I had to give up my education, I still want my sister to achieve her goals. I never want her to have to do the things I've done to survive.

Hardcore took us to this little soul food joint he knew. It had a relaxed atmosphere and a good vibe. The food was to die for, and I had a feeling this would become my new favorite spot to eat at. There were so many choices on the menu, and I just knew I would have to come back a few times to sample all the things that caught my eye.

I must've thanked him a hundred times since we'd arrived. I had never met someone so nice. He was fine as hell too. If I were a little older and he was a little younger, I could see myself crushing on him. He didn't have to take us in, but he did, and I am going to do everything I can to make sure he doesn't regret his decision.

We spoke about plans over dinner. Hardcore said he had a few ideas for jobs I could do to earn some money. I knew I needed a real job, but for that, I had to have some form of identification. Hardcore mentioned to me that he could help me with all of that. I just needed something which said I was eighteen, and then I could get a job. I would save as much as possible over the next few months and get a little two-bedroom apartment for me and Affinity.

When I got into my queen size bed later that night, I couldn't believe how lucky I was to have met Yanni that day in the store. I don't know where I would be right now if it weren't for her. Wherever it was, I was sure I wouldn't have my sister with me still.

* * *

The next few months were amazing. I quickly got Affinity settled into a new school. Yanni was teaching me the routes for the deliveries I had to make. I learned them quickly and hoped it would be this easy when I was on my own. I didn't want to seem ungrateful, but I needed that ID so that I could get another job too. When I mentioned it to Yanni, she just said that he would get it, but she wasn't saying when that would be. The only issue I had was with some of the other girls who came around. For some reason, they all hated me, and it showed.

It was only about four months until my sixteenth birthday, and I had hoped by then that we could be in our own apartment, but without the fake ID, I would never get a job. I decided to approach Hardcore myself when he came in this evening.

As soon as I heard his car pull up, I ran down the stairs to heat up his plate of food and make his drink. I laid it out on the table with a pre-rolled blunt. When he walked in, he came straight into the kitchen. He looked like he had been drinking.

"Hey, Alizé. What you cooked today, ma?" he slurred as he walked toward me.

"I made you barbecue chicken, mashed potatoes, mac 'n' cheese, and collard greens. I poured you a fruit punch to wash it down."

"Damn, little lady, this shit is dope. You're gonna make a nigga very happy one of these days," he stated while digging into his food. "Come and sit with me and talk while I eat."

"I was hoping we could talk about the fake ID I asked you about. I'd really like to get a second job to save for an apartment. I mean, I love it here, and you've been so good to us, but I don't want to feel like I'm taking advantage of your kindness. You must want your space back." I laughed nervously.

He looked up at me, put his fork down, and took some of his drink before speaking. "Do you know what it is that I do?" he asked.

"Erm, yes, and I don't want to stop my deliveries for you. I just need something extra so that I can save more," I added nervously.

"You're sounding real ungrateful right now, ma. I brought you here, gave you a job and a home for you both, and you're talking about it's not enough. You work for me. There is no getting another job. If you want more money, then you need to take on extra responsibilities here."

"I'm not trying to be ungrateful. I really do appreciate you. I just don't want to overstay my welcome. Please don't think I'm not thankful for everything you have done for us. I really am."

"You don't even know how fucking lucky you are!" he spat. Now he was getting angry. "You were brought here to be a hoe, Alizé. I run drugs and hoes. I told Yanni to bring you here so you could work off some of the money she owes me. I was going to break you in and pass you around just like the rest of these little bitches you see around here. Why do you think they hate you? It's 'cuz they know you ain't have to fuck to earn around here. Those bitches all start off fucking. Doing the deliveries is the next step. You got to bypass that, but now you fucked up. The only reason you and that sister of yours ain't being fucked by hella niggas all damn day and night is 'cuz I liked you. Now you wanna come at me like I don't look after you. I'll show you exactly what your new job will be," he said, walking toward me and unbuckling his belt.

Hearing the comment that he made about Affinity temporarily clouded my mind, so it took me a second to register what was happening. There was no way that I could risk anything happening to my sister, so I knew I would have to think fast.

"Please don't do this. H, you don't have to do this. Please," I cried as he grabbed me around the throat and pushed me back into the counter. He pulled my tights down with one hand and started touching my virgin pussy. "Please don't. I'm a virgin. Please stop it." I begged him.

It was like he was possessed. He wasn't listening to a word I said. He picked me up and sat me on the counter. Standing between my legs with my whole pussy on display, he looked into my eyes.

"I have wanted you since I laid my eyes on you. You and your sister haven't been put to work like the rest because I wanted to keep you for myself," he said while caressing my face.

I had a decision to make and a split second in which to do it. It was either get down or lay down, literally in this case.

"I like you too. I thought you would never look at me, being that I am so young. I didn't know if I should say anything or not. I've never even kissed a boy before. I was scared. I don't know how to approach someone on something like that," I said shyly, trying to smile.

He kissed me slowly and tenderly. I had to admit it was nice. I really started getting into it until we heard the front door open. He pulled back, handed me my clothes, and told me to go down into his man cave.

I ran my half-naked ass toward the door. Just as I pulled it closed behind me, I heard Yanni.

"Yo, those hoes been working hard today, boss." She laughed, and it shocked me to hear her be so blasé about it.

"I need you to do a delivery for me. Go and link up with Darion. He's already got the parcel. I just need you to show him the address and introduce him." Hardcore spoke with such authority.

"Cool, I'll take Alizé with me for a drive," she replied.

"Na, she's out still doing a run. See her when you're back," he lied.

Two minutes later, he came down the stairs. By that time, I had put my clothes back on. He came and sat next to me on the sectional and pulled me onto his lap.

"Where were we before we got interrupted?" he said as he kissed me slowly again. This time, his hands were roaming all over my body. When he broke away, he looked into my eyes. "I don't want you to be scared, but it's either you fuck with me, or you get put to work, little lady. Which is it going to be?"

"I want you. Not because of what you just said, but I've liked you since I walked in here that first day. Now that I know how you feel, I don't have to worry about you not wanting me here. I'm sorry if I made you mad," I replied, staring down at my hands, not wanting to make eye contact with him.

His hand touched my chin, lifting my head so that I was looking at him. "Don't ever be shy around me, baby girl. I'm going to be your first everything. I so wanted to destroy that tight little pussy from the second I saw you, but I'll take my time with you now I know you're a virgin," he stated as he lay me down on the sectional.

Hardcore stood up and released his monster dick. Slowly, he pulled my jeans and panties down and looked at my pussy. Parting the lips, he slid a finger up and down the slit. Gently, he pushed a finger inside me, working it in and out slowly. he then inserted another finger and dipped both of them in and out, but this time more vigorously than he previously had. His thumb started playing with my clit, and I was getting wet. I didn't want to be enjoying what he was doing, but it felt so nice. Just when I was starting to match his rhythm, he suddenly pulled his fingers out of me and licked all my juices off them. When he covered my pussy with his mouth, I thought I would pass out. I had experienced nothing like it before. It felt so good. I just wanted to scream out loud. My eyes started to roll into the back of my head. My entire body shook as my first ever orgasm ran through my body, and I couldn't even focus. Hardcore leaned down over me and kissed me again while trying to put his dick inside me.

"Just relax, ok. It's going to hurt, but only until you get used to the size of this big thing. Then you will be bouncing on it like a pro," he instructed.

He placed soft kisses on my neck, and I relaxed slightly and opened my legs further, allowing him the access he so desperately wanted. I winced in pain as he shoved his entire length into me.

"Arggghhh!" escaped my lips, and I covered my face with my hand. He pulled my hand away and kissed me gently.

"You're doing good, baby. Just relax and go with it. Just a couple more minutes," he said as he stroked in and out of me with precision. "This tight pussy gone make a nigga nut quick," he said as the speed of his pumps increased.

He pounded away at me for another two minutes before

he let out a grunt, signaling that it was all over, as he pulled his dick out and released his seeds all over my stomach.

I shot up and ran into the bathroom to wash it off. When I had wiped my body down, I splashed some water over my face. When I looked up, Hardcore was standing right behind me.

"You couldn't even bring your man a cloth to wash off with first? Don't worry. I'm gone train you properly," he said as he slapped my ass and turned the shower on.

"Get in with me. Let me get some more of that pussy before I go out," he demanded.

Joining him in the shower, he picked me up and wrapped my legs around his waist. Plunging his dick back into me, he started bouncing me up and down. At first, it really hurt, but then I started to get into it and help by moving myself up and down, matching his thrusts. The heat of the water raining down on us only heightened the feelings I was having.

"That's my girl, bounce for daddy," he instructed while slapping my ass again.

This time he lasted a little longer but not much. Within ten minutes, I was out of the shower, having fucked and washed myself up after. I wasted no time drying my body and putting my clothes back on.

Hardcore came back into the room and sat down. "You made the right choice, ma. If you gone be my girl, you won't have to fuck no one else. Just make sure you keep daddy happy. That's your only job in this bitch now. I will leave you money for the things we need in the house and your expenses. You need to keep the house clean and cook dinner each night. Ya' heard?"

"Yes, daddy, anything you say. Thank you for everything you do for my sister and me," I said as I reached up to kiss him.

"I'll let Yanni know that you won't be doing the deliveries anymore."

"But how will I earn money?" I asked stupidly.

"You won't need any if you stick with me. Now go to bed. You can stay in your room, but I'll come to get you if I want more pussy." He laughed to himself as I walked away.

I didn't know what the fuck I was going to do now. I didn't want to be fucking men for money, so letting Hardcore have his way with me had seemed like the easiest option. Hearing that I won't even be doing the deliveries anymore had me feeling like I fucked up. If I weren't earning any money, then how the fuck would I ever get Affinity and me out of this mess I had gotten us into?

I went back to my bedroom feeling dirty and ashamed. As soon as I heard the door close and Hardcore's car pull out of the driveway, I got back in the shower and scrubbed my body until I was red. I was disgusted with myself and how easily I let him have his way with me but also for how much I enjoyed it. My brain was saying no, but my body was betraying me and screaming yes, yes, yes!

I never imagined that my first time would be like this. I had always pictured it being romantic, and with someone I loved. One day I might get that kind of love, but for now, I have to do what I have to do to survive and keep my sister safe.

CHAPTER 6

Affinity Washington

It's been six months since we came here, and I don't know what kind of shit is going on around here, but I don't fucking like it one bit. There are always young girls walking around the place, and I'm sure that man is having sex with them all. They think I don't know what is going on, but I'm almost thirteen. I may be young, but I'm not stupid. I want to ask my sister, but last time I made a fuss, she just told me I was ungrateful, and I should be happy to have a sister looking out for me.

Yanni is just as bad. She pretends she is Alizé's friend, but I've heard her on the phone with some man, telling him how it was easy to get my sister to do whatever she wanted. Our situation makes me hate my mother even more than I already do. I know my sister is doing her best but seriously, how the hell is she meant to support us? If I ever see my mother again, I swear I will kill her myself. If my daddy was here, then I know that none of this would be happening to us.

I don't know how, but I know I need to get my ass up and out of here quickly. I just want things to go back to how they used to be when my dad was alive. I know my sister is just trying to look after us anyway she can, but I can't help thinking she's being dumb where these people are concerned.

Ever since Alizé met Yanni, she had been doing stuff she had no business doing. I'm going to make it my mission to find out more about her and this fucked up old guy we're living with. He must be at least thirty, so I don't know what he wants a load of young girls around for. It's twisted as hell. He must be some sort of pervert.

The only good thing about being here is that I've made some good friends at school, and it feels good not to have to hide in the house. I told everyone that my parents died in an accident and my eighteen-year-old sister is my guardian, and we live with her boyfriend. It was the only thing I could think of to stop people from asking me questions. I love my new school. It's much better than the old one, and my friends are dope as hell.

It's only two weeks until my birthday, and I want to do something special. I had just been on the phone with my new best friend, Empathy. She was nagging me to have a party, but I couldn't ask my sister that. It's not like this was even our damn house, but I've been fronting ever since I got spotted outside the crib by a girl in one of my classes.

I finished getting changed and made my way downstairs to see my sister.

"Sissy, you know it's my birthday coming up," I started as I walked into the kitchen where Alizé was preparing dinner. Hardcore was in there, too. He was sitting at the breakfast bar, reading over some papers.

"Yes, Affinity, how could I forget?" She laughed. "I've been saving for months to get you a gift. I thought we could go out for the day shopping."

"Wow, thank you, sissy! You're the best!" I added, feeling happy as a kid in a candy store.

"It was going to be a secret, but as we're on the subject of your birthday, we may as well tell you. Your sister and I decided that you could have a small party over at the crib with a few of your new friends. Maybe fire up the grill and have a pool party. Just a few people, though, not too many," Hardcore stated from where he was sitting.

"Are you for real? Oh my god! Thank you so much!" I said as I ran over and gave my sister a massive hug, then did the same with Hardcore. "I have to go and phone my friends. Y'all are the best ever!"

I ran up the stairs excited as a kid on Christmas Eve. I had to phone my friends and tell them the news. Maybe it wouldn't be so bad here after all.

Picking up my phone, I went into my call list and selected Empathy's number. She answered on the first ring.

"OMG! You're never going to believe it!" I sang into the phone.

"What! Tell me!" she replied.

"I'm having a pool party. I can only invite a few people, though, and I'ma need a new swimsuit. Shall we go shopping this weekend? I've been saving all my lunch money for weeks."

"Hell, yes, friend! This pool party is gone be off the chain! We need to make sure we're on fleek! I'm going to ask my dad for some money too," she said, making me feel slightly jealous.

I missed my daddy more than I let on. I was always a daddy's girl, and life has never been the same without him. I can't stand my mom for how she left us like we were nothing. I could feel myself getting upset, so I made excuses to Empathy and ended the call, letting her know that I would see her the following day.

I flopped down on my bed and started scrolling through Instagram on my iPhone X when there was a knock on my bedroom door.

"Come in," I called, expecting it to be my sister. I was shocked when I saw it was Hardcore. "Oh hey," I said, sitting up straight on my bed.

"Can I talk to you for a minute?" he asked.

"Sure. Did I do something wrong?" I questioned, as he never came to this side of the house.

"No, of course, you didn't. I know you're excited about your birthday, but I don't want your sister to get upset about how much it's going to cost. So, tell me what you need," he asked as he came in and sat on the chair in the corner of my room.

"Well, I was hoping I could get a new swimsuit and an outfit to wear. If it's not too much I'd really love to have my hair done too,. I was thinking we could use the speakers outside and get some meat for the grill. Will you cook?" I asked nervously.

"That sounds good to me, baby girl. Anything that will make you happy," he said, peeling off some money from a wad that he pulled out of his pocket and handing it to me.

"Thank you so much! You're the best. Erm, there's one other thing. I kind of told my friends that we lived with you 'cuz you're my sister's boyfriend. I hope you don't mind, but I didn't know what else to say when they asked why we lived with you," I added.

"That's fine, baby girl. I would love that to be true," he said, winking at me and leaving the room, closing the door behind him.

I picked up the money and counted it. He had left me five hundred dollars. This is more money than I have ever had to spend. I couldn't believe it. Wait 'til Empathy found out! This would be more than enough to make sure I looked the best I could on the big day.

I picked up my iPad and started looking at clothes online

until my sister called me downstairs for my dinner. I sat with her and talked for a while. It was good to see her looking happier than she had been in recent weeks.

CHAPTER 7

Alizé

I was pissed as hell that this man thought it was ok to tell my sister she could have a damn party for her birthday. Where the fuck does he think I am going to find the money to fund that shit when he just took my damn job from me?

I would have to get Yanni to let me sneak and do some drops while he was out of town this weekend. There was no other way for me to get any money.

Thinking of Yanni, she had been acting really salty around here recently. I made a mental note to check on her when she came in. I've been spending more time in the room with Hard-core, or H, as he prefers to be called at home. Things aren't as bad as they could be, and although I never would've chosen this life, I've been trying to make the best of the dire situation I'm in. Like I said, it's either get down or lay down. I chose the latter for an easier life. Judge me if you want to, but what was I supposed to do?

Don't get me wrong. He looks after me good. Life here could be so much worse, considering the business he is in. I just don't like that I have to ask him for money every time I want to buy anything, and he always wants to know where every cent has gone. He is so controlling and always had to have things a certain way, but as long as I follow his rules, everything runs smoothly.

I laid the food on the table and called H to the kitchen so he could eat. I wanted to speak to him alone, but even after all these months, his ass scared the hell out of me.

"Hey babe, I wanted to speak to you about Affinity's birthday. Are you sure it's a good idea to let her have a party? It's going to be expensive, and I'm not sure I can afford to do that as well as buy her a gift. And it's going to be noisy as hell with all those little girls running around the place."

"I told you to stop worrying about money. I got this, and little sis deserves the world. You just plan it and try to enjoy the fact you don't have to worry about a thing."

"Thank you, daddy. I've never had someone look after me the way you do. I'm not used to having nothing to worry about," I replied honestly.

"Well, you need to get used to it, my love. I've booked you an appointment at the salon tomorrow. It's gone be an entire day of pampering, just for you. You spend too long worrying about everyone else. It's time to enjoy some time for you. I even got you a new one of them Kindle things you like so much."

I thanked him again and kissed him passionately. I walked to the stairs and called Affinity down for her dinner. Just as I turned to walk away, the front door opened. Turning around, I saw Yanni stumbling through the door. My girl was looking a hot mess, and I could smell the liquor on her breath from six feet away.

"Hey Yanni, you're just in time for dinner," I said happily.

"Oh right, now you wanna know me. Where were you when I needed you? You ain't been around. You been too busy up under your man to even check me these days. Don't act like you're my friend, now bitch. Most times, you can't even return my call," she sassed with an attitude.

"Yanni, what the hell is your problem? You've been acting like a real bitch recently, and I don't need your fucking attitude!" I snapped back just as my sister came down the stairs, and H came out into the foyer looking mad as hell. Yanni's ass quickly shut the hell up when she saw him standing there.

"Do we have a problem here, ladies?" he quizzed while walking to position himself between us. "What's all that smart shit you were just spitting, Yanni?"

"Nothing, it's not important," she mumbled.

"No, ma, don't fall back now. Keep that same fucking energy you just had when you came in here running them dick suckers to my woman. If you don't like it here, I could always send you back to my brother. If we have an issue, let's talk about it?"

"No, it's fine. I'm sorry, Alizé. I just had a bad day. I shouldn't have taken it out on you. I'm just going to go upstairs."

"That's what I thought! Don't come back in here with that attitude again, or your ass will be on the first bus out of here."

H walked back into the kitchen, with Affinity trailing behind him with a shocked look on her face. I'm assuming it's because she heard him call me his woman. It sounded weird as hell to me to hear him say that. Our relationship was supposed to have been a secret until I was old enough to tell people without them thinking he was some kind of sick pervert. I know what everyone will think, but I've really started to care about him over the last few months. I think I would even go as far as to say that I was falling in love with him. The only thing that really got to me was that he was so damn possessive.

I didn't know what was wrong with Yanni, but I've got too much on my mind to even worry about her. I'm panicking really bad right now. My period is almost a week late, and I'm scared to even tell him. Luckily, he'd been away for a few days, so I told him that I'd had my period like usual. With Yanni acting up, I really have no one to turn to, and I don't know what I will do. Being a sixteen-year-old mom isn't a part of my life plan, but hey, neither is being the captive, secret girlfriend of a man twice my age. We don't always get what we want, though. Shit, in my life, I don't ever get what I want.

The Following Week

The day of Affinity's birthday came, and it was an enormous success. H acted like the perfect gentleman the entire day. We let the party continue until ten o'clock, and then the parents came to pick the kids up. The last one to leave was Empathy. Hardcore went out to attend to some business, so it was just me left with the two girls. She was waiting for her brother to come and pick her up, so I waited outside with them talking. He was taking his sweet time coming to get her. It was almost eleven o'clock by the time his ass pulled up.

"That's my brother's car," she said as she saw him approaching. He pulled up in front of the house with another guy in the passenger seat.

When he got out of the car and walked toward us, I swear I thought I would pass out. When our eyes met, my heart skipped a beat, and I heard the voice within telling me *this is the one*. It wasn't the expensive clothes, the ice he was wearing, or the flashy car, but something about his aura drew me to him like a moth to a flame.

He wore his hair in waves so deep that you could get seasick if you looked at them for too long. His eyes were almond-shaped and slightly slanted, giving his baby face a sexy look to hit. His caramel skin was smooth, and apart from a small amount of stubble, he was clean-shaven. As he stood in his tight white Gucci tee, I could see every muscle in his arms and chest protruding. Standing at around six feet tall, he was medium build, muscular but not too big, and he was fully in proportion for his size, judging by the dick print in his joggers.

"Yo, sorry I'm late, girls. I had some business to deal wit'. Happy birthday, lil' sis. Here, hold this." the guy said while handing my sister some money and hugging her.

"Thanks, Knight," Affinity said, hugging him back. "This is my sister, Alizé."

"Hey ma, thanks for having big head here over today. I hoped they behaved themselves. Y'all better not have had no little niggas out here with them today," he said while extending his hand to shake mine.

"Hi, nice to meet you. And yes, they were fine. They had a good day," I replied. I don't know why, but I was nervous as hell around this nigga. He was the finest man I had ever seen. I had to stand with my legs crossed just to stop my juices from flowing down my thighs.

"Right then. We better be out. I need to drop your ass off and head back out," he said to Empathy. "It was nice to meet you, Miss Alizé. I'm sure we'll see each other again," he said, with a wink of the eye and a smile on his face.

"I'm sure we will," I said shyly.

Affinity and Empathy hugged each other goodbye. Watching their interaction warmed my heart to know that my sister had made a real friend in Empathy. It was nice to meet her friends today, and it's reassuring to know that she has settled in well here.

As I turned with my sister to walk back inside, she looked at me, grinning.

"I see you flirting with Knight! He's fine, ain't he?" She giggled.

"Affinity, what the hell you know about fine with your little young ass? I said, pushing her playfully.

"I know he's more your age than your *man* is!" she sassed back.

"H is a good man, and he cares about us. He looks after us really well, and age ain't shit but a number lil' girl," I countered.

"Hmmmp, well, let me come home with a twenty-something year old boyfriend and see if you still sing that song."

"Try me if you want to, sister. You and that nigga will be dead with quickness."

"I love you, Alizé, and thank you for today. Tell H the same when he comes in. I'm going to bed. Night."

"I love you, too, sister. Sleep well." I watched her walk up the stairs and headed into the kitchen to ensure it was all clean before I went up to bed.

As I busied myself around the kitchen, I couldn't shake the feeling that I got when I met Knight. Never in my life have I wanted to get to know someone as much as I wanted to know his fine ass. He was easily the finest nigga I had ever met. He didn't look too much older than I was, and he was obviously getting money. I wish I were free. All I wanted was to earn my own money and have nice things in my life. Ever since I was a little girl, I just knew that I wanted a good career and a nice house. I would have my own before I met the man who I wanted to spend my life with. I vowed to never be like my mom, relying on a man for everything. Just thinking about her made me mad. She just walked out the damn door one day and didn't come back. I hated that woman for how she did my daddy. Even now, I still couldn't believe that she'd been fucking the man that killed him. She had a good man who loved her and looked after her. I would never understand why someone would fuck it all up for sex.

I took myself upstairs to shower and re-do my hair before Hardcore came home. He liked for me to look on point at all times. I walked into his room. Well, I suppose it's our room now since he made me move all my stuff in there a few months ago. I pulled out one of my new silky nightshirts that he liked for me to wear, with nothing under it.

Walking into our bathroom, I stripped out of my clothes and went into the cabinet under the sink to retrieve the pregnancy test I had hidden there yesterday. I ripped the packaging off and sat myself down on the toilet. I wiped myself, then got up and washed my hands. Placing the test on the side, I said a prayer that I was wrong.

I picked up the test and looked in the little window. Immediately, I sunk to the floor and cried.

Pregnant.

CHAPTER 8

Knight Carter

I wasn't too happy about my little sister being in that house. I don't know the nigga that Affinity's sister is with, but she looks hella young compared to his old ass. I just don't know what a man that old wants with a chick that damn young. At first, when Empathy asked me if she could go to this little party, I put my foot down and said no. Flat out, she wasn't going, but then her little ass started crying, and she knows that will win me round each time. I can't stand to see baby girl cry. Growing up with absent parents like ours, it was like we only had each other sometimes. There was me, my brother Supreme, and Empathy. We were all that mattered. I went hard for both of them. It's not like we didn't have money when we were kids. Shit, money is the only thing we did have a lot of the time. My parents were so wrapped up in their own lives that they hardly made time for us growing up.

"Fine, you can go, but I swear you better call me if anyone moves funny around you. And if that old ass nigga has any of his old ass friends there watching all you girls, your ass needs to leave straight away. Ya' heard?" I warned. "You know I don't play about you, little sis. I'll shoot that nigga and his damn mama behind fucking with mine."

"I know you will, Knight. It's not that serious, though. Affinity's my best friend, and I can't miss her birthday party. You know I'll behave myself, and if anyone says anything or even looks at me then I'll phone you to pick me up. Can I have some money, though? We want to go shopping before the party starts." She laughed with her hand out.

When I met Alizé, though, I got to admit. She was a cool chick. I felt safer letting my sister be there, knowing she was there the whole time, but I still couldn't help thinking that something wasn't right with that whole setup. Looking at her today, I'm certain that she is younger than I am. I don't know what could've happened in her life to make her end up with someone like this Hardcore nigga, but I plan on finding out. I'd been looking into this motherfucker, and I didn't like what I've heard about him. I'll make a point to question my sis in the morning and see what I can find out.

Empathy, or Emi, as I always called her, jumped in the back seat of the car, and we sped off in the direction of home, but first, I had to drop my boy off round the corner. I had to get her back and then head out to the traps and collect the dough, and then I was planning to slide by this chick's crib and hit that once or twice before I headed home to lay it down.

The chick I was seeing tonight was Natalia, some hot little shawty from the city's north side. She was cool as fuck, but I already knew she wanted something I just wasn't prepared to give her right now. I was a sexy, young, get-money nigga. I didn't want to be tied down. I never lied to these bitches, though. They all knew what it was. When I was with them, I was with them, but when I wasn't, then I was single to do whatever or whoever the fuck I wanted. There was plenty of time for settling down with someone. Having kids and shit like that will come one day, but that's the motive for me right now. I want to stack my paper and move up in the game.

I didn't want to have a relationship like my parents did. They were so consumed with their petty tit for tat arguments and consistently trying to 'one up' each other that they barely made time for us kids. We were lucky that our nanny and housekeeper, Mrs. Audrey, was there. She was more of a mom to us than our own mother. Even though we were all grown now, she was the one who welcomed us home each day and cooked for us each night. I couldn't tell you the last time my family ate a meal together. The three of us kids always made time to see Mrs. Audrey every day, though. I don't know who I would've become if it wasn't for her love and support over the years.

My father spent most of his time at work or at his condo downtown, usually with his side hoe. He thought none of us knew about her, but I had seen him with her more times than I care to remember. I would feel bad for my mom, but I know her ass cheats on him, too. I don't understand why they just don't divorce and move on with their lives. Instead, we live in a world of lies and deceit. We have this picture-perfect family to the outside world, but no one knows the truth of the fucked-up situation we lived in.

My mother spends all of her time traveling and living her best life. She has been out of the country for three weeks, and my father hasn't even noticed that she's gone. All my life, it's been the same way. They fight, then one or both of them would leave for days, even weeks on end. My oldest memory is one of them having a huge fight. After that, my mom disappeared for six months. Not a single word to anyone. She came back with baby Supreme as if nothing had happened. My father was happy as hell to have another son to show off to the world. That's all we were to him... accessories to show off with.

I vaguely remember hearing my father say that she had

been having an affair with someone. Over the years, in arguments, my mother has screamed about the man with whom she had an affair. From what I overheard, my father killed him, and my mother has always told him that she hated him for killing the man who she claims was the love of her life.

Every time they are in the house together for more than five minutes, they end up fighting. Then one of them walks out, and the other tears shit up a bit and goes too. It got to the point that we all just hoped that both of them stay gone. Life is easier this way. As long as Mrs. Audrey receives her check, the bills remain paid, and our allowances are sent each week, then we really don't need either of them selfish motherfuckers around us. I don't know what kind of parents couldn't just put their differences aside for the sake of their children.

I just knew that when I finally settle down, it will be with one woman. I don't know why a nigga needs a side piece. Marry the woman that is your best friend, and you will never need another woman in your life. Shit, I was gone wife a bitch with a thing for wearing wigs. That way, I would feel like I got a different bitch every damn day.

I pulled up to the crib and took Emi inside. As usual, there was no sign of life in this big ass crib. Mrs. Audrey was the only person in again. That poor lady must get lonely in here. Now that we're all older and have our own lives, she is by herself most of the time. I was going to make a point to discuss that with her. This was her home, and she could invite anyone she trusted over here to chill with her. She has the entire guest house to herself, but she will stay in the room next to Emi's when my parents are both away.

Pulling out my phone, I phoned Reme to find out where his ass was. He knew his curfew was eleven o'clock, so that little nigga should be here by now. He had been giving all kinds of problems since he linked up with this new little girlfriend of his. Her useless ass mama lets her stay out 'til all hours and never has no clue where the fuck she is or what she be doing out in these streets. The kid is fifteen, and she is asking for her to get knocked up with that kind of attitude. Well, I can tell you it won't be my damn brother that gets trapped by the local thot. No sir. I make sure that little nigga got protection on him at all times. It ain't like my damn pops will ever be around to talk to the boy. I had to teach my brother and my sister the ways of this world. And my way was to always have your own back first and foremost. Don't get me wrong, I'll do anything for my homies, but I ain't trust no one a hundred percent, except for myself. Even your own shadow leaves you in the darkness.

* * *

On the drive over to collect the money from my traps, my mind wandered back to Alizé. There was something about that girl that spoke to my soul. She was cute as hell, but there was a sadness behind her smile that never fully reached her eyes. I can see just from how she holds herself that she has been hurt. She appears a lot older than her age, and I'm sure that has to do with whatever situation led her to be groomed by that sick fuck. Call it what you like, but that's what it is.

Once I collected the dough from the five traps I had around these sides, I left and headed north to go and check Natalia. Natalia was a cute lil' redbone chick who I met outside the store one day when I dropped my homie off. I could tell she was older because she let it be known that she wanted some of my young ass right off the bat. After fucking around and chilling for a minute, I found out that she was twenty-seven. At just seventeen, my young ass thought I hit the jackpot. This chick taught me a few things, and I don't mind admitting she had me hooked for a hot minute with all the sexual encounters we were having, but now it's her ass who's hooked and trying to make me settle down.

When I pulled up outside her crib, it was in darkness. I got out and used the key she had given me to let myself in. I called out to her, but there was no answer. I took off my sneakers and hung my jacket up. I quietly walked toward the bedroom in search of Natalia. I stopped outside the bedroom door when I heard giggling. I pushed open the door to her bedroom, and I was shocked as hell to find her naked in the bed with her best friend, Liah. These older bitches were clearly drunk and freaky as fuck.

"Hey baby, you took your time. We kinda got started without you." She giggled as she crawled to the edge of the bed.

Straight away, she started pulling at my belt, trying to free the beast that I was working with. I let her carry on while peering over her at her friend, who was now lying back with her legs spread, playing in her pussy. I just shook my head, knowing this was going to be a long night. As soon as Natalia pulled my dick out, she had her thick lips around it. She swallowed my shit within seconds and started bobbing her head up and down to match the rhythm of her hand that was jacking me off at the same time. I leaned forward and slapped her ass, while never breaking eye contact with Liah. Nat's head game is A1. I bit down on my bottom lip and watched my dick disappear into her mouth while listening to the wet sounds of her friend's juicy box. I was harder than a motherfucker right now and needed to slow down the pace before I shot my seeds all down Nat's throat. I pulled my dick out of Nat's mouth and started stripping my clothes off.

I grabbed the blunt behind my ear and lit the tip.

"Let me watch you two for a minute," I said as I took a seat in the chair in the corner of the room and watched the show that these broads were putting on for me.

Nat crawled back toward Liah and pulled her legs apart as wide as possible. Slapping Liah's hand out of the way, she replaced it with her own. Slowly, she started touching all over her friend. Then she stuck her ass out and went in headfirst. She was licking and sucking like a pro, and I knew it wasn't the first time these two had gotten freaky together. Liah had her hands on Nat's head, guiding her to where she wanted her. Nat looked up at her friend seductively, licking her lips.

"Turn that ass around," Liah panted.

Nat quickly positioned herself back between Liah's legs in the sixty-nine position. Both women wasted no time attacking each other's pussy with their mouths while both trying to look at me at the same time. I'd had enough of watching. Putting the blunt down, I stood up and walked toward the bed stroking my dick.

"Let me in there now."

"Which hole do you want first, daddy?" Liah purred.

"Get that pussy over here, ma," I ordered Liah while laying back.

She straddled me and moved slowly so she could adjust to my size. Nat moved so that she was positioned in front of Liah with her ass toward me. She started sucking on Liah's titties as she rode me. I inserted two fingers into her hot dripping box and moved them at the same speed as Liah was bouncing up and down. This shit was enough to make a nigga want to bust within minutes. I tried to think of anything other than what was going on in front of me right now, but all I could think about was Alizé, and that shit had me nutting even quicker. I pulled out, and Nat caught all my seeds in her mouth.

Liah jumped off and let Nat take her seat on the throne.

After a few more hours and a few more rounds, I was spent. The three of us fell asleep intertwined in each other. I made it a point never to stay overnight because, as I said earlier, I didn't want to lead her on.

I eased out of bed, grabbed my clothes, and went into the bathroom. I brushed my teeth, had a quick shower, and put my clothes back on. When I went back into the room, I noticed Liah was gone. I left some money on the side for Nat and made my way to the front door. Stopping to grab my sneakers, I noticed Liah sitting in the kitchen. When she saw me, she came to where I was with a piece of paper. When I opened it, there was a phone number.

"I had a good time last night. Call me if you want to hook up," she flirted as she sashayed away. I just shook my head and stuffed the paper into my pocket before leaving out the door. I couldn't believe the night I had just had.

CHAPTER 9

Yanni

After the little argument I had with Alizé a few weeks ago, I've just been keeping to myself. I've been making as many deliveries as I could just to be out of the house. It wasn't supposed to be like this, and now I'm just stuck in the same fucked up situation I was back home with Man-Man.

Hardcore hasn't even looked at me since he's been fucking with that little bitch. It's not that I'm jealous of their relationship, but as she is quickly learning, fucking with the boss has its perks. Now I'm back to having to do runs just to pay off a debt which isn't even mine to fucking pay, thanks to that bastard Man-Man. Then to top it off, I get a message from Hardcore this morning telling me I must attend one of the parties tonight. I would usually be happy to party, but this wasn't that kind of party. It was a sex party where a bunch of Hardcore's fucked up associates would pay to come and fuck a number of teenage girls.

The girls were all either runways or were down on their luck like Alizé was when I met her. I lured them all in, and now seeing how broken some of them were, it was starting to eat away at me. I never really felt guilty about the shit that I made them do until recently. It's as if all of a sudden, I've grown a conscience, and I want to get far away from here, but I have nowhere to go and nobody I can turn to.

For the time being, I'm back to fucking to get by, and being that Hardcore doesn't want me anymore, I had to have sex with every random ass man he told me to. What none of these motherfuckers know is that I have been cutting the product to make it stretch further. I add some shit to it to bulk it up and then keep the rest to sell without anyone knowing. I only add a little 'cuz I don't want to get caught out, and the regular customers will tell if the product isn't as good as it usually is. I was saving up to get as far away from here as possible. My life would be nothing more than what it is now if I didn't get out of here somehow. My plan was to make Hardcore fall in love with me so he would look after me, and I wouldn't have to do this shit anymore. However, I really fucked up by letting Alizé come here. That bitch stole my shine, and now he's all up under her ass.

I couldn't wait until his ass went away next week, and I got some peace. When he wasn't here, I just palmed all the work off on one of the others, and I wouldn't have to do much. I was shocked to see Alizé sitting alone in the kitchen reading over some papers.

"Hey," I said while looking in the refrigerator for something to eat.

"Hey Yanni, how's things?" she said.

"Good. What about you?" I asked.

"Yea, I'm ok. I've been meaning to speak to you, but you haven't been around much."

"Ok, so what did you want to talk to me about?"

"I wanted to know if you needed any help making some deliveries while Hardcore is away this week? Don't tell him, though. Please keep it between us like the old days."

"Hmmp, maybe. I'll see. Why don't you want him to know?"

"I just need some extra money for something, but I don't want him to know. Is that so bad? He doesn't need to know everything Yanni," she said with an attitude before she started crying uncontrollably.

I walked over to where she sat and pulled her into a hug. "What's going on, Zé? Talk to me."

"I'm pregnant, and I don't want to have the baby, but if I tell him, he will go crazy! Please help me! I need to make the money to have an abortion while he's away. I will be sixteen tomorrow, and I can get the procedure done if you say that you're my older sister. I need your help, Yanni, please!" she begged.

"If he finds out I helped you do this, you do know we will both be dead bitches, right? Shit, Zé. You can't have a baby, so we really ain't got no choice. He should be happy you're doing this. Hardcore's ass would be in prison if anyone found out he got your young ass pregnant, anyway." I decided I would help her, but I was using the situation to my advantage. Being nice to Alizé now would be beneficial to me in the long run.

We came up with a plan, and I was gone let Alizé hit the deliveries hard with me to earn the money so we could fix her problem. What she didn't know was that she would only be delivering the product that I was cutting off the top. I just needed to stack as much as I could so I could escape this hellhole.

When Hardcore came in later that night, I left them to it and went up to my room. As I walked away, I could hear him questioning her about what we were talking about. I knew she wouldn't tell him anything 'cuz it would fuck up her chances. Alizé knew as well as I did that I was her only chance of being able to get rid of the baby. Part of me thinks she should keep it; I know I would. At least then, he would look after them both for the rest of their lives. She would be set to rake it in through child support from a nigga that's paid, but it wasn't my life.

* * *

The next morning, I woke to the sound of a car horn outside the house. Looking out of my window, I couldn't see where it was coming from, but I just knew it wouldn't end well for whoever was making all that damn noise. I went and brushed my teeth, then pulled my robe around me and went downstairs.

When I got to the bottom of the stairs, the front door was already open, and I spotted Affinity outside. Walking out behind her, I could see Hardcore and Alizé looking at a new Lexus CT with a massive bow on it. Alizé was jumping up and down like a little kid. Just as I stepped onto the porch, Affinity turned to look at me.

"Oh, hey Yan. Did they wake you too?"

"Yea, what is all this?"

"Alizé's sweet sixteen gift. It's dope, ain't it?"

"Hell yea, it's dope. Nice wheels, Zé."

"I know, right! I love it! Thank you, daddy!" she said as she turned and thanked H again.

I don't mind admitting that I was feeling jealous as hell just looking at how happy she was. That was supposed to be me. Hardcore was supposed to fall in love with me. I really put in the work trying to make him see it, but it's like as soon as he saw her, he was blind to anyone else. Mark my words, he is gone wish he'd seen me.

My mama used to tell me you catch more flies with sugar than with shit. So, I was going to be nice to both of them right now, but as soon as I was ready to, I would expose both of their fake asses.

I left them all to it and went to get myself ready for the

day. H was leaving this afternoon, meaning we would be having a meeting before he left to listen to his orders for the week. I made sure to look extra cute today, so I pulled out my True Religion shorts with an off-the-shoulder cropped sweater. I curled my twenty-six-inch weave and left it loose. Slipping on my new release J's, applying my MAC lip-gloss, and putting on my Gucci shades, I was ready. I was just going to be hitting the deliveries and hanging on the block, so this would be perfect.

When I got into the kitchen, Alizé was cooking breakfast with the biggest smile on her damn face. Shit, I would, too, if I got a car this morning. Hardcore looked me over and licked his lips. Standing up and tugging at his crotch, he turned to me.

"You ready to go over your work for the next few days, Yanni? Come down to the man cave, and I'll show you the paperwork. How long 'til it's ready, baby?"

"It'll be about twenty minutes. I'll shout when it's time," she said, as he walked toward her. He kissed her hard, palming her ass at the same time. He nodded his head toward the basement door, and I turned to walk down the stairs.

The minute he got me in his man cave, he started.

"What the fuck you got them little ass clothes on for? Are you trying to wind me up, Yanni? You out here trying to give niggas what belongs to me? Bring yourself on over here and let me show you who still owns that sexy little ass," he said while pulling his monster dick out and bringing it to life.

"We can't do that with Alizé just up there. What if she catches us?" I stated while slowly walking toward him.

He roughly pulled me into his embrace. Hardcore had his hands roaming all over my ass while he was kissing my neck. "You must be doing this for attention. If you don't want to get caught, you better get this nut quick, girl. You missing daddy's dick, huh? Feel this big motherfucker. He's dying to be up in that tight wet box."

He turned me around, pulled my shorts down, and slapped my ass. "Grab your ankles," he ordered in a low voice.

I quickly grabbed hold of my ankles and braced myself for that daddy dick. He started rubbing my entrance with his big mushroom head and poked it in slightly, moving it in and out slowly until his dick was coated in my cream. He grabbed my hips and went in full force, pounding away at me mercilessly until my legs started to shake.

As I tightened my muscles around his dick, I could feel it start throbbing inside me. Bouncing my ass back as hard as I could, I was trying to get that nut before Alizé caught us and all hell broke loose. Within minutes, I felt his entire body tense up. He was so caught up in the moment that he didn't pull out like he usually does. He skeeted his whole load all up inside me. Rushing to the bathroom, I grabbed him a hot washcloth and made out like I was going to clean myself up. I locked the bathroom door, turned on the taps and lay myself down on the floor, and lifted my ass to make sure it went all the way up there. I wasn't one to look a gift horse in the mouth. I was keeping the gift he just gave me and praying the seed grew. If I'd known it was that easy, I would've been parading around here half naked the whole time.

CHAPTER 10

Alizé

When I went outside and saw a new Lexus CT in the driveway, I didn't think anything of it. H has hella cars parked out there all the time. It was only when I walked to the front of it and saw the huge pink bow on the front that I started to question it. Never in a million years did I imagine it was for me. When he came up behind me with the key, I almost passed the fuck out.

"Happy sweet sixteen, baby girl. I pulled some strings and had someone copy your mom's signature. I managed to get your driver's license, so you're free to drive, baby, but remember, I've got eyes everywhere, so don't be out here acting a fool just because you got a lil' bit of freedom. It can be taken away as quick as you got it!"

"Thank you so much! You can trust me, I swear!" I said as I reached up to kiss him, ignoring the fact that he just gave me a gift and threatened to take it away in the same breath. Everything comes with conditions, even me being allowed a bit of freedom, but I wasn't going to complain.

I went back inside to prepare breakfast for everyone before Hardcore went away. He had some business to tend to in

Atlanta, so he would be gone for the next five days. That should give me enough time to earn enough money so I can get the abortion before he gets back.

As soon as Yanni walked into the kitchen and I saw what she was wearing, I wanted to ask her to watch how the fuck she dressed in front of my man. Her ass was hanging out the bottom of them tiny ass shorts she was rocking. They were so damn short the pockets were hanging down lower than the bottom of the fucking shorts. They think I'm stupid, but I peeped the way H was watching her ass as she moved around the kitchen. When he called her down into his man cave, I just knew I had to try to listen in. I stood right up near the door, trying to hear what they were saying, but it was no use.

Just as I was about to open the door, I heard my sister running down the stairs, so I dashed away from the door. I didn't want to get caught eavesdropping on them and look like I was stalking them in my own home.

I don't know whether it's just my hormones or there is something I should be concerned about, but I was not about to let anyone bump me from my spot... not even Yanni's snake ass. I knew I had to fight to maintain my place at the top of the tree, just until I managed to get enough money together to leave his ass once and for all. I may be young, but I'm not stupid, and ain't no one coming along and taking my place because I am not being subjected to the shit these other girls have to go through, and neither is my sister.

When they came back up to eat breakfast, I watched both of them like a hawk. I was trying to see if I could spot any signs of anything between them, but they both had good-ass poker faces. I made a mental note to watch them both moving forward. As soon as Hardcore finished eating, he kissed me goodbye and left for his meeting, after which he was going straight to the airport. The fact that he left without trying to get any pussy was suspect as hell to me. Usually, his ass tries to fuck before he leaves the house and when he gets back.

Yanni came in and told me that if I drive her 'round all day, then she'll split her money with me. I knew that I would get this money in no time, so I used her phone to book my appointment for three days' time. I had been putting little bits of money away, and I already had half the money I needed.

Me and Yanni rode around all day delivering the product. It felt good to be young and free for a few hours. By the end of the first day, she gave me a hundred and fifty dollars. We made our way home, just in time for H to call me. We spoke for five minutes, and I could swear I heard a bitch in the background before he abruptly ended the call.

* * *

The appointment came 'round quicker than I expected, and before I knew it, I was sitting in the waiting room with Yanni for them to call me back to see the doctor. The blunt that we had smoked on the way over here had me in a daze. When the nurse came out and called my name, Yanni turned to me and asked me if I was sure about going ahead with this. I knew I had no option but to go through with the abortion. I never thought I would be in this position, but I also knew that I could have nothing tying me to this man. When I was ready to leave him, it had to be a clean break. As I lay on the table, letting them perform the procedure, I thought about all the things that led me to be in the situation I'm in right now. I let the tears fall silently with thoughts of my daddy invading my brain. He would be so ashamed if he could see me now. There ain't no way I should be going through this shit. One day I will avenge his death and get my own revenge on the bitch who birthed me, but right now, I'm just fighting to survive.

It was over pretty quickly, and before I knew it, we were

on our way back home. As soon as I got in, I got straight into my bed and cried.

I couldn't believe what my life had become. If you had asked me a few years ago, I would've told you that at sixteen, I would've been thinking about school and what college I wanted to go to, not sitting in my bed crying because I had to have an abortion and being scared of the man who'd been holding me captive finding out. Yea, in front of everyone, I act as if I love Hardcore, but the truth is, I can't stand his sick pervert ass. I have to play the game to keep my sister safe, but I'm just biding my time until I can leave.

I didn't hear from H that day, which I found strange because he usually calls and messages me constantly when he's out. I was glad that he left me alone. It was a well-needed break from him and his bullshit. I don't think I had it in me to pretend I gave a shit today. I curled up in bed with my Kindle, downloaded some new releases, and tried to forget everything. I searched around until I found his stash and rolled myself the fattest blunt possible and smoked the entire thing while reading. Sleep found me easy after that. I was high as fuck and enjoying every second of it without having to look over my shoulder constantly like I did when H's bipolar ass was around.

* * *

When I woke up the next day, it was almost three in the afternoon. Looking at my phone, the only messages I had were from my sister, saying she was going to have dinner with Empathy, and one from Yanni letting me know she had left me some food in the oven and to call her when I was awake. I was shocked that I hadn't heard anything from Hardcore, so I sent him a quick text before I went and showered. I had been in bed for a whole twenty-four hours, and I felt nasty as hell, having only gotten up three times to use the toilet.

I went in search of the food that Yanni had left me, hoping it was something nice 'cuz I'm so hungry I could eat a horse. I kept checking my phone, but there was still no reply from H. I decided I would go and meet Yanni and get me some weed. I knew that if I smoked too much of Hardcore's stash, he would notice, and he doesn't like for me to smoke unless he is here with me for some stupid reason.

After meeting with Yanni and chilling for a while, I decided to head home for my sister. Just as I pulled up into the driveway, I saw a car pulling in behind me. I looked in my rearview mirror and noticed that it was Knight's car. Checking my face over, I got out of the car to greet them.

Knight got out of the car with my sister and walked toward me.

"Nice whip, ma. This new?" he said.

"Yea, it's a birthday present. I love it."

"Well, happy birthday, ma. So, I was thinking about taking these big head little girls to Six Flags before they go back to school. You down?"

"Yea, they will love that."

"I want you to come too. You know, in case they need the restroom or some shit," he said quickly while looking me up and down.

"Ermm, when?"

"Shit, we can go tomorrow if you're down."

"Yea, ok, that would be cool," I replied, knowing full well H would be big mad over this but fuck him right now.

I haven't heard a peep from him since he left, so what he doesn't know won't hurt his ass. He hasn't even phoned me or sent a message in days. I'm not pressed, though. He can do him and let me do me. Plus, Knight is fine as hell. He's the kind of nigga I should be with. Someone nearer my own age, and I feel like he would be fun to be around. I guess we'll see tomorrow. It's been years since I went to Six Flags, too, and Affi and Emi will love it.

"I'll come by and pick you both up at ten, and we can make a day of it."

"Ok, sounds fun. I'll see you in the morning."

With that, Affinity and I walked back into the house. Seeing as it was just the two of us home tonight, I decided I would use some of the money that H left to order us a pizza. We sat and watched movies all night, just like we used to.

CHAPTER 11

Knight

Lil' Mama has been on my mind heavy these last few weeks, so I was happy as hell that Affi needed a lift home tonight and I was more than willing to drop her. That's lil' sis, though, so I would always make sure she was good. But there is something about her sister that makes me want to be around her. I don't normally fuck with chicks that are that young. I usually go for the older ones. Or should I say, they go for me. I tried to get some info out of Affi on the ride over without making it obvious that I was feeling her sister. I found out that lil' mama just turned sixteen, which means she is only a year and a half younger than I am, so it's not too much of a difference. Emi had already told me that Affi lives with her sister 'cuz their mom just walked out one day and left them to it. Their dad got killed, so it was just the two of them in this world. That alone made me want to protect them. It's a cold world out there not to have people in your corner. All I know is that lil' mama done a good job keeping them both out of the system, which is probably how she ended up with that old clown that she's with.

I decided to take them all out tomorrow to get to know

her better. I know she's got a man, but I don't care. Dude is mad older than her. It doesn't even make sense that she would be with someone like him. I asked one of my homeboys who lived over on their side about him. He was in the car with me the night I picked my sis up from there. I wanted him to show me what crib the dude lived at. It turns out this old cat is a hustler, and rumor has it he runs chicks up and down the country. I just hope he ain't had Alizé doing shit like that, or it wouldn't matter how intrigued I was by her. I would dead that shit and move on to the next. She still seems to have some innocence about her, so I don't think she has been out there fucking for money.

Since I was out, I stopped by the traps and see what was good. For a young nigga, I was moving up the ranks in this game. Thanks to my pops, my name already held weight in these streets. I only fucked with my niggas, though. I ain't putting no new niggas on. Just me and my day ones be running this shit. My crew consists of me, my cousins, and our homeboys from grade school. The only new people that came on board had to be blood with one of us. In this game, too many people get fucked up by trusting the wrong motherfuckers.

I swear Drake said that shit best.

No new niggas, nigga we don't feel that. Fuck a fake friend, where your real friends at? We don't like to do too much explainin,' story stayed the same through the money and the fame. 'Cause we started from the bottom, now we're here...

Ever since that night with Natalia and Liah, they've both been blowing up my phone. So, I did what any young nigga would do and shared my free time between them both. The only problem is that Nat doesn't know about me hooking up with her girl, and I doubt she would be overly impressed, but that wasn't my problem. She shouldn't have opened the door to let that woman in the bedroom with us. Shit, she should've known that after one taste of this dick, every chick is hooked. I knew it wouldn't end well, so I would have to stop fucking with one or both of them eventually, just not today.

* * *

The drive out to Six Flags wasn't that bad. The two girls were hella excited and sitting there talking shit like they usually do. It was good to see that my sister had a real friend in Affi, which made me happy. Most of Empathy's friends were only her friend because of who she was. They either befriended her for status, money or just to say they were friends with someone in the infamous Carter family. Even though I know Alizé ain't got dough like that, Affinity always looks good, she always has money for her lunches, and she doesn't expect anything of my sister, other than friendship.

The whole drive over there, Alizé kept checking her phone.

"You expecting a call, ma? You ain't stopped looking at that phone since you got in the car."

"Erm, no, it's nothing. Sorry, I didn't mean to be rude. So, tell me something about you, Knight."

"Well, I'm the oldest, and other than big head back there, I have one more sibling, my brother Supreme. I try to keep them both on the right path. What about you? What brings you to this crazy ass city of ours?"

"I wanted a fresh start after my daddy died and mama left. I have a friend who lives here, so I packed our shit and brought us here," she answered.

"Sorry to hear that about your pops. That's fucked up that your mama left. So, it's just you taking care of Affi?"

"Yeah. Well, my boyfriend takes care of us both, if I'm honest. I had plans of going to school, but with things how they are, it's just something that will have to wait for a while. Making sure this one has what she needs comes first to me."

"You're a good person. I can tell just by the way you stepped up for your sister. If you ever need a job, just holla. My pops got a few businesses. I might be able to hook you up."

"Thanks. I'll keep that in mind if my current job doesn't work out."

* * *

I haven't had fun like that since I was a kid. Emi and Affi had a great time, too. Even Miss Alizé relaxed after a while. We stayed all day, right until the park closed. I never wanted to leave. Just being around Alizé was enough for me right now. She was like the breath of fresh air I needed in this cold world. I could see such pain in her eyes, but I knew that given the chance I would be the one to take all that pain away.

"Yo, I had fun today," I told her as we drove to get some food on the way home.

"Me too. Thank you for today, Knight. You don't know how much I needed to let my hair down a bit."

"Look, I know you got your situation and shit, but I hope we can be friends. Ya know, kick it sometime without these little big head girls eavesdropping on everythin' we saying. Ya feel me?"

"Yeah, I'd like that."

The girls wanted pizza for dinner, so we went to this little spot I knew on the South Loop. They sold some of the dopest deep-dish pizza Chicago had to offer. I couldn't help but notice how Alizé had tensed up at dinner. She was more relaxed earlier on the scary ass rides than she is now. I tried to ask her what was wrong, but she just tried to play it off like it was nothing. One thing she would have to learn if we were going to be friends is that I don't like to be lied to, but I'll let it go for now.

I dropped Alizé and Affinity back at the crib and headed home with Emi. I was just going to lay it down for the night and take a well-deserved break. I phoned my bro, and he said he would be home soon too, so we planned to have a movie night and spend the rest of the night, just the three of us, chilling. We were so used to it being just us kids that this was our idea of a family night. I couldn't help but send a message to Alizé. It had been a long time since I'd had a chick on my mind so heavy, and I ain't even got the pussy. I had to laugh at myself, but I knew something was drawing me closer to her, and I wasn't going to stop until she was mine. Right now, I'm just going to be her friend and get to know her a bit better, but mark my words, that niggas days are numbered.

It felt good to chop it up with my brother and sister for the night. Usually, we would ask Mrs. Audrey if she wanted to join us, but she was in the guest house with her friend. We told her that she needed to enjoy her life and now that we were older, she could allow herself a bit more free time. Since our parents are hardly ever here, that poor woman doesn't feel like she can take a day off from work. I booked her a vacation for two people for ten days in the Bahamas, where she is originally from, so she can go back home and see her extended family. I would stop by my pops' condo in the morning and tell him that either he or my mother needs to be here more for Emi.

* * *

I pulled up outside my pops' secret crib that he thought we knew nothing about, but I know where he and my ma both go when they're not at home. I exited the elevator and knocked at the door. I was going over what I wanted to say while I was waiting for an answer. I wasn't shocked when a woman answered the door.

"Hey, I'm looking for my pops. Can you tell him I'm here, please?" I said as I walked straight past her and into the condo, leaving her to close the door behind me.

"Oh, erm, yes. Sorry, one minute," she stuttered as she walked off to get my pops. I made myself comfortable on the leather couch and waited.

"Hi son, what are you doing here?" he asked as he walked into the room. I stood up to shake his hand, as he taught us to do at an early age.

"I just came to check on you. It's been a minute since you came home. I sent Mrs. Audrey on vacation, so either you or ma will need to be home to check on Emi a bit more."

"Ok, son, well, that woman deserves a break. She is a life-saver. I'll increase her pay, too. I'll speak to your mother, and we can arrange something for Empathy."

"You're not going to introduce your friend, pops?" I said, nodding my head toward the woman who was now in the kitchen area, making herself busy.

"This is Serena. We're old friends. Serena, come and meet my oldest son, Knight."

"Hi Knight, it's lovely to meet you. I've heard a lot about y'all," she said chirpily. I returned the gesture with a head nod. No words were needed, I just wanted to know her name.

After kicking it with my pops and discussing business for an hour, I made my excuses and left.

CHAPTER 12

Alizé

These last few months, Hardcore has hardly been at home, which is good for me, but it's making me feel like I need a job more. Affinity is back at school, and with him hardly ever here, I'm going out of my mind with boredom. I've even been out doing deliveries with Yanni more and more, just to get some money.

I've been talking to Knight a lot, too. He is a breath of fresh air to me in this miserable existence I call my life. So far, he's been a perfect gentleman, but I can tell he wants me as much as I want him. He is everything to me, and honestly, apart from Affinity, he is the only good thing in my life.

Despite the fact that he is never here, Hardcore still rules me with an iron fist. He wants to know where I am or what I am doing all the time but can't even answer as to when he is coming back. If he calls me and I'm not home, he doesn't stop ringing until I'm there. Once I'm at home, I won't hear from him for hours, sometimes days.

I had just finished cleaning the house when I heard the front door open. Thinking it was Yanni, I went downstairs to greet her. I was shocked as hell to see some woman that I didn't know standing in the foyer.

"Can I help you?" I asked.

"Yes, I think you can. Alizé, right?" she said with her hands on her protruding stomach.

"Yes, who are you?"

"I'm Hardcore's wife, and I want to know what the fuck is going on."

"His wife?"

"Yes, little girl, his wife, and the mother of his four children. And seeing as he won't tell me the truth, I was hoping you could. How long have you been fucking my husband? And how fucking old are you?"

"I'm not a little girl, I'm almost seventeen, and I didn't know he had a wife or children."

"Sixteen!!! A fucking child! My husband has been sleeping with a fucking child. Our daughter is fifteen. He's fucking sick! What kind of man does that? I thought you were older. How long has this been going on?"

Just as I went to answer her, Hardcore came crashing through the door.

"Baby, it's not what you think. Let me explain. I told you my cousin Yanni was staying here while trying to sort her life out. Well, this is her friend, and she needed somewhere to crash. Nothing is going on between us," he stressed while glaring at me. "Right, Alizé? Tell her there is nothing for her to worry about."

"Don't fucking lie to me, you bastard. I've heard the calls to her and the way you speak to her. I've seen you tracking her car and watching her on the millions of cameras you have hiding around this place. You're obsessed with her. She is barely older than your daughter, you sick, perverted motherfucker. I want you out of my house today. This shit is fucking over. I want a fucking divorce!" she screamed.

He backhanded her straight across the face, causing her to fall back into the wall.

"There ain't no divorce, sweetheart. It's 'til death do we part, remember? Get your ass up and take yourself home. I'll be back later to remind you who's in charge since you must've forgotten. How many times do I have to tell you about that mouth of yours?"

She quickly scurried out the door. He watched as she pulled off and closed the door.

"She is right. I have been watching you. Give me your phone, so I can see who you've been spending so much time talking to."

"It's just my friend from back home, that's all."

"Don't fucking lie to me, Alizé!" Hardcore roared as he came toward me looking crazy. He grabbed me by my throat and slammed me into the wall. "I'm sick of you bitches keep forgetting your place. I run shit around here, not fucking you, not Yanni, and not that dumb bitch of wife of mine."

"How could you sleep with me knowing she is pregnant? I can't believe you're married with children! So, everything we had was all a lie? I thought you cared about me?"

Whappp.

I didn't see the first slap coming. He dropped me to the floor and started hitting and kicking me like I was a nigga in the streets. I couldn't do anything to protect myself. I just curled up in a ball and cried. It felt like the beating I was getting went on for ages. The entire time, he was screaming at me. He said he knew about the abortion, the deliveries, and even me spending time with another man. He warned me what would happen if I gave his pussy away. I was pleading with him to stop. I swore up and down that I never slept with anyone other than him, but his crazy ass wasn't trying to hear anything that I had to say to him.

He dragged me up into the bedroom and ripped my

clothes off. Pushing me on the bed, he spread my legs as far as they could go and rammed his monster dick inside of me. I swear he tore my shit in two the way he rammed it in me with such force and no lubrication. He continued raping me for the next three hours. I just lay there, watching the clock go 'round and 'round.

When he finished, he demanded I go and get myself cleaned up 'cuz he was taking me somewhere. He told me to make sure I looked good and not take too long. So, I hurried my ass up so as not to make him madder than he already was.

When we got in the car, he picked up his phone to phone someone to tell them we were on the way. I wanted to ask where we were going, but after earlier, I was scared, so I just sat in my seat quietly.

* * *

We pulled up outside a nice-looking house, which had four cars in the driveway. He got out and started walking toward the front door.

"Whose house is this?" I asked.

"Don't ask me no fucking questions. Just get in here and do as I fucking say, for once," Hardcore spat back.

I walked into the house behind him. In the living room were four men that I had never met before.

"This is our new recruit, Alizé. She has a problem doing as she is told, so I thought you guys could help me make her a little more obedient if you catch my drift," he stated with a laugh. "Same room as last time?" he asked one of the men.

"Yeah, fam, same room. Just take her back there, and I'll be in to go first," his friend said while eyeing me up and down.

Hardcore grabbed my hand and led me into a room at the back of the house. There was a bed and a side table on one side and a chair on the other.

"Get in here and take your clothes off, now!"

"Why? What are you doing? Please don't be like this, baby. I'm sorry. Can we just go home and sort this out?" I pleaded.

"This is what happens to disobedient bitches. You need to be taught a lesson. I've been spending too much time away, and you must've forgotten who the fucking boss is around here! Take them off Alizé, or I'll do it myself."

"You have a fucking wife. I'm allowed to be angry. Please, can we just go and talk about this? Please, baby, don't do this."

Hardcore slapped me so hard my head flew backward. He followed up with a punch to the stomach. Grabbing me, he pushed me down on the bed and tore my clothes off me.

"If you don't shut the fuck up, next time, it'll be your sister. Now be a good little bitch and do what daddy says."

Nothing could've prepared me for what happened next. Tying my hands to the bed frame, he let each of his friends rape me, and each time I begged them to stop, but each time Hardcore came back to the bed and slapped the shit out of me. In the end, I just lay there and take it. I cried the entire time in fear that they would do this to Affi. H just sat in the chair watching. I thought he loved me, but how do you do that to someone you claim to love? It was bad enough to find out that he had a wife and kids, but this is a joke.

I almost had enough for a small apartment, but it would take me a few more weeks of running with Yanni until I had the amount that I needed. I just pray that I make it through without being subjected to this shit again.

* * *

When we left the guy's house, we drove home. I stayed silent the entire time. I had no fucking words for this man. He could fuck himself. The second we pulled up at the house, I got straight out of the car before he even had the chance to put it in park. I ran straight into the house and upstairs to my bath-room. I stripped my clothes off and got in the shower. Turning the water up, so it was scalding, I lathered up my washcloth and started scrubbing my body. I used the entire bottle of my Bath & Body Works dark kisses body wash, and I scrubbed and scrubbed, but still, I didn't feel clean. I stayed in there an hour, just scouring my whole body. My skin was red and sore by the time I went to get out, but just as I put my foot on the bathroom floor, the door came flying open.

"Get back in there. I want some pussy," he demanded.

"I'm sore, H," I complained as I tried to walk past him.

He grabbed me by my hair and dragged me back into the bathroom. "Did I fucking ask you if you wanted it? Just do what the fuck I said and get your fat ass in there. You ain't learned yet that your life is better when you do what daddy tells you? Listen up, bitch. You do what I say when I fucking say it, and you do it with a fucking smile. You don't see the others walking around here in their feelings, do you? Shit, even Yanni's feisty ass wasn't this fucking bad. You have a good life. I provide for you and your sister. I look after you both, let you live rent-free in this big ass house, plus I got you a damn car. Bitch, I treat your ass better than anyone you ever met, so you need to show some gratitude and stop being ungrateful. Now come suck on this big thing and make it hard so I can fuck you."

I felt deflated. I didn't even have any fight left in me. I just did as I was told, dropped down to my knees, and took his dick into my mouth. I knew my head game was A1, so it wouldn't take but a second to get his nasty ass hard.

"Ahhrrghhh, that's its baby," H moaned with his eyes closed as he held my head and fucked my face. I wanted to be sick from where he was thrusting his dick into my throat that hard, but each time I gagged, the more turned on he got.

Thoughts of cutting his dick off invaded my mind. *I've got to find a way to get the fuck out of here before this shit kills me.*

Pulling me by the hair still, he stood me up and dragged me into the shower.

"Put your hands on the wall and stick that ass out for me."

Doing as I was told, I braced myself for his dick. He used to make me so wet, but now my pussy was dried the fuck up at the thought of him. I didn't need to worry myself with that 'cuz this sick bastard pulled my cheeks apart and rammed his dick into my ass. I cried out as the pain shot through my entire body. It hurt so badly that my legs buckled from under me. He was holding onto my hips and going in harder than he ever had when he fucked my pussy.

"Damn, this little asshole feels good. Baby, this shit is tighter than your pussy was the first time I fucked you," he kept talking and slapping my ass. I was in so much pain that I cried out, begging for him to stop. With a grunt and one last stroke, he came inside me. Straight away, he let my hips go, and I fell to the floor. Hardcore got out of the shower, leaving me there in a heap on the floor. He walked out without looking back.

I sat there for a few more minutes, crying. It was like the floodgates had opened. I cried over the state of my life, the fact that I failed my sister by bringing her here. I cried for my dead daddy and cried over the fact my hoe ass mama left me to deal with all of this shit alone. If I ever see that bitch again, I'ma forget she birthed me and rip her fucking head off her damn shoulders for how she did my sister and me. I fucking hate my life so much, and if it weren't for Affi, I would just end it all right now.

CHAPTER 13

Knight

Six Months Later

I was getting more concerned for Alizé. Emi and Affi came to me the other day and asked me to speak to her. They say she has gotten really withdrawn and is hardly leaving her room unless it is with the old cat. Affi has been spending more and more time here with us, which is cool, but I can't help but worry about Alizé. From what I'm told there is some shit which just ain't right over there, and I'm not going to stop until I find out what the fuck it is.

We had become real good friends. We were talking daily and messaging all the damn time, and then suddenly, she stopped all contact with me. I asked the girls why, but they just said she wouldn't say and that I should respect her decision. What kind of shit is that? I'm still really feeling her, and usually, I wouldn't be sweating it, but something is stopping me from giving up on her completely. She ain't got much more time before I just say fuck it and forget her altogether.

The more time Affi spends at our crib, I can't help but notice how much she and Emi look alike. At first, I thought it was because they always wore their hair the same way, acted the same and dressed alike, but the more I watched them, the more I noticed that shit.

When my pops came by the house the other day, I noticed that he kept looking at them together. I know he could see it, too. I could see it in his eyes. When he heard her name, I saw a flash of recognition in his eyes. There can't be too many kids called Affinity out there. I know my pops, and I know he knows her, or he knows of her.

I couldn't think about all that shit right now. My nigga Sway is getting married next week, so tonight is his bachelor party, and this shit was gone be lit as fuck. My niggas were known to get wild as fuck out here when we were out party-ing, and it's been a minute since we all kicked it and popped some bottles.

As soon as we walked in the building, the DJ started shouting.

"Yoo, we got the Legion in the building tonight! Shout out to my nigga Sway, about to be a married man. All you chicks better make my nigga's last night of freedom the best night of his life!"

We all gave a head nod. It seems like the whole damn city was out to party with us. We had hired out the whole VIP section, and I'd paid the baddest strippers to be giving my nigga lap dances all night. Shit, this is his last night to party as a single man, and it's down to me as his best man to make sure he sees enough ass and titties to last him a while. Later, we're having an after party in the presidential suite at the Astoria, and only the baddest of the bad will be invited to party with the crew. It was my aim to make sure my nigga had the best night possible.

We got a hundred racks of dollar bills delivered earlier. Everyone knew that when the Legion came out, it was raining hard up in here. The crew was popping bottles and chucking bands all around the damn place. Sway was enjoying all the ass and titties he was getting in his face, looking like a kid in a candy store.

* * *

As the club started winding down, Sway took his pick of the chicks he wanted to come joins us in the suite, and we made our way to the after party. We had another thirty bottles in the room already. The tunes were pumping, and everyone was having a blast.

About an hour into the party, someone was knocking at the door.

"Yo, it's the hoes. Bro is gone finish tonight right. I got him six bad bitches that he can do what the fuck he wants to," Sway's brother boasted as he got up to open the door.

I just had to shake my damn head at this fool. I would never in my life have to pay for pussy, but Sway would fuck anything, which is why none of us can believe his ass is the first to jump the broom.

In walked four chicks. I looked them over and turned back to the chick I was talking to. It took my mind a second to catch up with my eyes. My head snapped back around when I realized one of the bitches was damn Alizé. I pushed the chick off my lap, walked straight up on her, and grabbed her by the arm. She looked like she wanted to piss on herself when she realized it was me.

"What the fuck are you doing here, Zé?" I snapped at her.

"Um, I um. I can't talk to you right now, Knight. Just pretend you don't know me, please," she stuttered as she quickly turned away and joined the girls she had arrived with. By now, they were all doing shots and sniffing lines of coke. I couldn't believe my eyes watching her like this was normal behavior for them.

I went and sat back down with a fresh bottle and started

drinking that shit straight. I pulled out my Swishers and a sack of weed and started rolling. The whole time I was watching her, my face was screwed the fuck up while she was smiling and joking like it was fucking normal to have men pawing all over her.

As they started pairing off and going into rooms, I stood up and walked over to her.

"How much for this one?" I asked the bitch who was taking the money.

"Two hundred," she replied, holding her fingers up like I needed help to count or some shit.

I pulled a roll of cash out of my pocket and handed her two-hundred-dollar bills. Pulling Alizé behind me, we went into one of the rooms. As soon as I closed the door, I grabbed her and pushed her up against it.

"What the fuck is going on, Alizé?" I spat angrily.

"You wouldn't understand. I have to do this to protect myself and Affinity. He made me, and I have no other option. I can't lease an apartment until I am old enough. I have no one I can turn to. He is the only person who looks out for us."

"You're coming with me. I'm not taking no for an answer either. Affi sure as fuck isn't going back to that old pervert's fucking crib, and neither are you."

"He'll find me and punish me again. That's why I had to stop speaking to you. You don't know what he did to me last time, and he said he would kill both of us if I spoke to you again. Please, just forget about me and let me go before they find out something is wrong."

Just as the words left her mouth, there was a commotion outside the room. I could hear a man's voice and the look on her face told me it was that sick, old motherfucker.

"Let me get you out of here, Zé. You don't have to do this. Just let me help you."

"You can't help me, Knight. No one can. I've got to do

this. It's the only way to protect Affinity," she stressed, as she messed up her clothes and hair while pulling my shirt out and undoing a few of the buttons. "Make it look real," she urged as she opened the door to the room.

"There you are. I was looking for you. I need you and Dalia to fix yourselves up. You have another appointment to get to if you're finished here," he said while grabbing her arm and pulling her closer. I noticed the way she flinched when he reached for her.

"Actually, bro, I was hoping to keep this one for a few more hours. How much?" I said calmly.

"You can have her until morning for a rack," he said cockily.

"Cool," I said, pulling out my wad of cash and counting out a rack to hand to him.

"Be home by ten, Alizé. Remember, I can find you wherever you go," he whispered, thinking I couldn't hear him.

"Yo Knight, I need to speak to you before you leave," my homie, Wrapz, called out from the other side of the room.

"Knight?" I heard the old cat say. "You didn't learn your lesson last time with this nigga, huh Alizé?"

I turned my head around, and Hardcore had Alizé by the hair, and his strap pointed at me. Within seconds the entire Legion had their straps upped and aimed at this nigga's head.

"This won't end well, my g. I suggest you put that shit down. You 'bout to look like some Swiss cheese up in here nigga. I can assure you my hittas don't miss. They on target every damn time," I said, not giving a fuck.

"I'll see you in the streets, young gun," he said with a head nod. "Come on, girls. We're leaving." Never lowering his gun, Hardcore started to back out of the room.

"You can bet on it, blood," I said as I watched him leave.

I was in no mood to party after that, so I made my excuses and headed home.

* * *

When I got in, I knocked on Emi's bedroom door and waited for a reply. When they didn't answer, I decided not to wake them and just talk to them in the morning.

Going into my room, I stripped my clothes off and went into the shower. Turning the water on and the temperature up, I stepped inside. I let the water fall all over me and let my mind go back to Alizé. I couldn't fucking believe this nigga was pimping her ass out like that. He was one sick mother-fucker. I knew I needed to get Affinity out of that fucking house before he does some sick shit like that to her. I don't know how, but I plan to get a DNA test done on her after seeing the way my pops reacted when he met her. I just know that she is kin to me. The results don't matter because either way, she's moving in here, and I don't care what anyone has to say about it.

After spending twenty minutes letting the hot water wash away some of the stress in my head, I got out and went into my room. I pulled out some blue Dior boxers to put on and then climbed in my bed. Picking up my phone, I checked my messages. As usual, Liah and Nat had both been blowing up my line. Plus, this new chick I had been talking to, but not a word from the one person who I hoped had reached out. Feeling frustrated as hell, I pulled a blunt out of my drawer and took the whole thing to the face before falling asleep.

* * *

When I woke up, it was almost eleven o'clock. I never slept in this late. I went into the bathroom to brush my teeth, then went into my closet and pulled out some basketball shorts. I found a fresh wife beater and my slides before making my way down the stairs.

"Hey, dumb and dumber," I joked as I walked into the kitchen where Emi and Affi were. "Morning, Mrs. A. How you doing today, beautiful lady?" I asked, walking up behind Mrs. Audrey and hugging her.

"Chile, go sit your ass down and let me bring you some food," she ordered as she swatted my hand away from the food she was preparing.

"So, what do you girls have planned for today?" I asked.

"Shopping if you give us money," Emi's cheeky little ass said.

"I should probably head home later. I haven't been back there in days," Affi added.

"You're not going back there, Affinity. You're moving in here with us. I thought we could get your bedroom fixed up for you. You can have the room next to Emi's so you can be together still. Please don't fight me on this and leave your sister to me. Once she realizes I'm not letting you leave, she will have to listen to what the fuck I have to say. I don't want either of you going to that house again. That nigga ain't right in his head."

"I can't leave my sister on her own. I'm all she's got," she whispered.

"I know shit has been hard for you both these last few years, but you're not alone anymore. I've got you both. Zé is gone be moving in, too. She just doesn't know it yet. I found out some shit that I'm not happy about, and I refuse to let either of you stay there any longer. Go and get dressed so we can go shopping."

I'm happy that neither of them decided to fight me on it, but it didn't matter if they did 'cuz my mind was made up. The hard part would be getting Zé to agree, but if I had to kidnap her little ass, I would.

CHAPTER 14

Alizé

The minute we got into the car, Hardcore turned and slapped me so hard that my head hit the window. He was hitting and punching me, and I just knew this was going to be a long ass night. When we got back to the house, he dragged me inside by my hair. Tracks were coming out all over the damn place where he was ripping them from my head. When we got inside, he continued to beat my ass like a nigga in the street. This wasn't even my damn fault, but after tonight I'm sure Yanni's ass was setting me up. It was her client who invited us to the party, and it's not like she doesn't know who Knight is. She met him outside the crib when he picked Affi up.

It's not a coincidence that Hardcore turned up right after I went in the room with Knight, just like it's not a coincidence that he found out about me doing deliveries with her. I'm certain she phoned him and told him to come there. She was always jealous of my relationship with him. When I found out that she brought me here to make it easier on herself, I knew she was a fake ass bitch.

Hardcore beat my ass for hours. By the time he finally stopped hitting and kicking me, the sun was coming up.

"Go and get yourself cleaned up. You look a fucking mess. Make sure the house is clean by the time I get back here, or I'ma fuck you up," he threatened as he kicked me one last time before walking off and leaving me in a heap on the floor again.

I tried to pull myself up off of the floor, but my body hurt so fucking bad. I couldn't move more than a few feet before the pain was too bad to move any further. I just lay there thinking about the hundreds of men he'd made me have sex with within the last year and wondering what would become of me.

* * *

I must've passed out from the pain because when I woke up the sun had started to set, and the room was getting darker. I spotted a light under the bed. It was my phone. I tried to crawl toward it, clinging to the last bit of hope that I had. I needed someone to help me. My body had never hurt as much as it did at this moment. The phone lit up again as I struggled to reach it while praying that Hardcore didn't come back.

When I finally reached my phone, I grabbed it, and when I saw Knight's name on the screen, I knew that if I could just get through to him, I would be ok. I waited while the phone connected and started ringing. When he didn't answer, I felt defeated. I tried him two more times before nearly giving up. Just as I took the phone away from my ear to the end the call, I heard his sweet voice booming through the speaker of the phone.

"Zé, where are you? Are you ok?" he said frantically.

"I need your help! Please help me!" I broke down crying to him. In this moment, he was the only person I could think of that could save me. I just hope he doesn't hate me after finding out the truth about me.

"I'm coming right now, baby. Don't worry. I got you."

Just hearing those words made me burst into tears. I could hear him calling my name, but my head was so heavy, and I couldn't move my mouth to answer him. That was the last thing I remember before it all went black.

* * *

When I woke up, I didn't know where the hell I was. I tried to sit up, but I couldn't. My body was so sore. I turned my head and spotted Knight sleeping in the chair next to the bed that I was in. I looked around the room and realized that we were in some sort of hospital. There were machines all around me and wires attached to various parts of my body to monitor my heartbeat. I moved my hand to get the bottle of water that I could see on the table, but I knocked it off, waking Knight in the process.

"Don't try to move, baby. Just stay still. Let me get the doctor," he instructed as he kissed my forehead.

I winced from the pain that I felt. Less than a minute later, he came rushing back into the room with a doctor behind him.

"Well, Miss Alizé, I'm glad to see you awake. You started to worry us all. Just stay still so I can take the tube out of your throat," the doctor ordered.

Once he was done, he handed me a glass of water, and I downed it in one gulp.

"You've suffered a lot of injuries. You're lucky your boyfriend found you when he did. A lot of the damage is superficial, but you do have some internal injuries which are concerning but I'm certain that you'll heal just fine without any lasting damage, but I'll expect to see you again for follow up appointments. The police will want a statement about what happened, and any details of the women who did this to you." he left out of the room leaving just me and Knight. He came and raised my bed, so I could sit up a bit.

"You scared the shit out of me Zé baby. I thought you weren't one make it ma." He said as he kissed my forehead gently again. He sat next to me on the bed and pulled me in close to his chest.

We sat in silence for a few minutes, just holding each other. He spoke first.

"You know that you're not going back there, right? You and Affi are moving in with me, and I don't care who don't like it. Don't even try to fight me on this. I'm gone help you get your shit together. I already ran it past my ma and pops but neither of them are hardly ever there, so you won't see much of them anyway. It's just Emi, my brother and Mrs. Audrey. You'll love her; she used to be our nanny when we were young but now, she's just like our second mom. Shit she is more of a mom than the woman who birthed us ever was."

I had never heard him be so open and honest about his family.

"Thank you, Knight. You saved me; if you didn't come and get me, I could be dead right now. What would've happened to Affi if I died?"

"As long as I live, I got you and Affi. I'll never let anything bad happen to you again. I'll be there to protect you."

"You really are my Knight in shining armor. Thank you."

"Na baby, I'm your Knight in body armor." He said with a chuckle.

He pulled me in close and we fell asleep in each other's arms. No one has made me feel this safe since my daddy was alive.

* * *

The next day, the doctor told me I could leave, but I had to take it easy for the next few weeks. It would take around six to eight weeks for all my injuries to heal, but the results of my blood tests would be back soon to let me know if I had gotten any STIs after being forced to fuck all of them people. I was embarrassed as hell that Knight knew all of that about me and that he had told the doctors.

When we got to Knight's house, I was amazed. I've never seen a crib this nice in my life unless it was on the television. After introducing me to Mrs. Audrey, Knight took me to what I assumed was a guest room until he opened the door. I was shocked to see the whole room was in a black and gold theme and all my things were there. I turned back around to look at him.

"How did you get all of my things?" I asked, feeling confused.

"Come on and sit down," he said, helping me onto the bed. He sat down on the other side of me before continuing.

"The night I came to get you, I got my crew to meet me at the crib in case anything kicked off. When I walked in and saw what he had done to you, I can't even describe how mad I was. Seeing you like that fucked me up, baby girl. You were barely breathing and completely unresponsive. I picked you up and carried you out to the car so I could get you to the hospital. Just as I put you in the car, that old nigga turned up. I sent you to the hospital with two of my niggas and went to address that fuck nigga.

He was outnumbered, being that he only had that bitch Yanni with him, and I was there with half the fucking crew. We dragged them back into the crib, and I fucked them up the way they fucked you up. I was mad as hell after seeing how he did you, but it's ok. You ain't ever gotta worry about either of them sick motherfuckers again. After making that bastard feel my wrath, I knew I needed to get to you, so I got two of my niggas to empty you and Affi's rooms and lit that crib the fuck up. All your shit is here. I ain't know what you wanted to keep, so I just brought it all. Oh, and the contents of that nigga's safe is in one of these bags too. You deserve all that shit and more after what he put you through. You're going to be secure here with me. I'ma protect you with everything I've got and make sure no one ever hurts you again."

I just sat there, not knowing what to say. Knight put his arms around me, pulled me close to him, and kissed my forehead. We just laid there in silence for a few minutes.

"Thank you for saving me," I expressed once I could find my voice.

There was a knock at the door and in walked Affi and Emi. I swear they looked more alike each time I saw them together. Both looked shocked when they saw me. I must've looked at a hot mess. I hadn't even seen a mirror yet.

"Sissy, we're so glad you're ok," they said in unison. Walking over to the bed, they both climbed up and hugged me.

"I was so scared that you would leave me, and I'd be all on my own," Affi admitted as she suddenly burst into tears. She lay with her head in my lap like she used to, and I stroked her hair.

"I'm never going to leave you, sissy. We're going to be ok now," I reassured her.

"No one will ever hurt any of you. I'll make sure of that. I'll die behind protecting mine, know that," Knight added.

Knight ordered some food, and the four of us sat on the bed watching movies and eating for the rest of the evening. It was perfect how something so simple made me feel so lucky. I was lucky to have made it out of there but even luckier to have my Knight in body armor protecting me. For the first time in months, I fell to sleep content. I don't know what the future will hold for me, but I actually think that I'm going to be ok for the first time since my daddy died.

When I woke up the next day, it was two o'clock in the afternoon. I couldn't believe I had slept that long. I went into my bathroom and looked around. There was a bag of toiletries, a washcloth, some towels, and a new toothbrush. I brushed my teeth and undressed. It was the first time I had really looked at my body since I woke up. Hardcore had really fucked me up, and there wasn't a single bit of my body that wasn't covered in red and blue marks or bruises. My once beautiful face was bruised and swollen so badly that I didn't even look like my damn self.

Stepping into the shower, I tried to wash my body the best I could, but I was in so much pain that I couldn't stay in there for very long. Luckily there was a bathtub, so I filled it up and put some Epsom salts and bubbles in before climbing in. After laying there for twenty minutes, I got out and went in search of something to put on.

Looking through some of the bags left there, I could see a lot of new clothes from expensive ass stores. I opted for some tights and an oversized sweatshirt. I pulled on some socks, and my slides, then put my hair up in a messy bun before trying to find my way to the kitchen.

When I found my way back through the maze to the kitchen area, Mrs. Audrey was in there preparing some food.

"Good afternoon, baby, how are you feeling today?" she asked as she walked toward me and hugged me.

"I'm a little better, thank you."

"I made you some food and got your medication for you. Sit down and try to eat. You came at the right time, too. I was just about to sit and eat a spot of food myself. So we can sit together and get to know each other a bit."

We sat and ate our food. Mrs. Audrey asked me about myself and told me she had never known Knight to be as worried as he had been the last few weeks. She explained that she had been in his life since he was a young boy, and she loved them all like they were her children. By the way she spoke, I could tell that she adored them all, and it was evident that Knight cared a great deal about her. I wish I had someone like her in my life. She is so pure and genuine.

After I finished eating, I took my pain medication and went to sit outside in the garden. Affi and Emi were swimming in the pool, so I went and sat down and watched them messing around. I love that my sister has a real best friend, someone who will always be there for her to talk to. Lord knows she must have a lot built up inside her. So much has happened to her in the last few years that I feel like I need to look into getting her a therapist. I don't want her growing up fucked up because of all the shit she had been subjected to in her short life.

I remembered what Knight said to me last night about the contents of Hardcore's safe being in one of the many bags around my room, so I got up and went back inside to see how much money there actually was. The total was over two hundred and fifty thousand dollars. I couldn't fucking believe it. I had never seen so much money in my entire life.

I stuffed it all back inside the duffle bag and headed outside to sit in the sun. Everything would be fine, and at least now I have enough money to get somewhere for me and Affi to live. As soon as I was healed, I would speak to Knight about his offer before of helping me get a job and try to get an apartment somehow.

For the next few weeks, Knight was doing everything he could to make sure I was happy and comfortable. I was really starting to care about him. He was the perfect gentleman, and he was the only man I knew that didn't want something from me in return. I just wish he didn't know what he knew about me 'cuz he would never look at me the way I wanted him to now.

CHAPTER 15

Ava Carter

When my son came to me and asked me if he could let these two little girls move into the house, I was concerned, to say the least. Not because I was worried that my son would get the older girl pregnant like most mothers of a teenage boy would be, but because I couldn't risk my children finding out the truth and having these girls around would most definitely lead to some secrets being exposed. Secrets that I've tried to bury.

Knight was stubborn like his father, and as soon as I said that I didn't think it was a good idea for them to live in the house, he made it clear that if they had to leave, then he would be leaving with them. I offered to let them have one of the apartments that I own. I could never see them on the streets, but I couldn't risk Chief finding them at the house, and while he still has access, he could turn up whenever he wanted.

As soon as he started talking about Alizé and Affinity, I knew it couldn't be a coincidence. There couldn't be two sets of sisters with those names. I knew I needed to go home and see what was really good. Hearing what they had been through these last few years made me feel so guilty. If I ever see that bitch Serena again, there will be a problem.

The second I laid my eyes on them, I knew. Affinity and Empathy were the spitting images of one another. Meek always told me he thought Affinity was my husband's child, and looking at her next to my daughter, it is evident that she is. However, Alizé looked just like her daddy, and her eyes were identical to his. Those same eyes I thought I would never see again. The same eyes I had stared into so many times. The eyes that made my heart skip a beat every time they roamed over my body. The same eyes that belonged to the love of my life, Meek Washington, the man that my heartless bastard of a husband had killed years ago in a rage of jealousy and brought me home his head in a duffle bag.

I hated Chief ever since that day and refused to be in the same house as him point-blank and period. I knew that if I had to be around him, I would end up killing him, and I didn't want to be the reason my kids didn't have their father too.

My husband found out about my affair with Meek and went bat shit crazy. He had some fucking nerve being upset over it, considering he was fucking that hoe Serena for years and still is even to this day. He thinks I don't know about them, but I've known about her living in that condo way before Knight found out. You see, whilst I fucking despise the man, he is still my husband, so I like to keep track of him and his hoes to make sure they don't interfere with my life.

"Hi, I'm Knight and Empathy's mom, Ava," I greeted when I walked into the garden.

"Hello, ma'am," they both replied in unison.

"Hey, ma," Empathy called from the pool, where she was swimming laps.

"Hello, darling," I called back. "I thought I should come by and introduce myself to our guests and maybe take you all out for some dinner. That is if you're feeling up to it, Alizé."

"No, she's not going anywhere. We can order in if you

want to have a meal with us all, but she's not up to going out. She needs her rest, ma," I heard my son chime in from behind me.

"Ok, grab the menus then, son, and we can order something. And ask Mrs. Audrey to set the table."

"No, it's her day off. She's gone out for the evening with her friends. Emi and Affi, you can dry off and get changed. Then you girls can choose what we eat, phone up and order it, then set the table. I need to talk to ma and Zé for a minute alone," Knight said, sounding like the young boss he is and making me realize I had lost all control in my own house. What was supposed to be a temporary break away to deal with my grief over losing the love of my life, Meek, had turned into the normal way of life. I knew I needed to fix it soon before it was too late.

He sat down at the bottom of the lounger that Alizé was resting on and put his hand in her lap.

"You ok, baby girl?" he said tenderly. The love between them already was evident.

"I'm feeling much better today. I've taken some of the painkillers that the doctor gave me, and I ate some food that Mrs. Audrey prepared for me before she left."

"I'm happy that you're feeling a bit better because I really need to talk to you about something. I was going to leave it until you were healed fully, but I've found out some information today, and I can't sleep on it. Ma, you need to hear this shit, too."

"What is it, Knight?" I asked, feeling petrified of the answer he would give me. I prayed that he hadn't found out that I was why this poor girl's daddy was dead.

"Haven't either of you noticed just how much Emi and Affi look alike?"

"I guess they do favor each other. What makes you say that? I asked him, while Alizé didn't respond.

"Well, I DNA tested them both, and it turns out that pops is Affi's dad."

"You fucking did what?" Alizé shot up but then winced in pain and sat back down. "How could you do that without even asking me, Knight?"

"I'm sorry, but I had to know. That's not all I found out, either. The woman I met at my pop's crib a few weeks back is your mom. You told me she was dead. Why did you lie to me, Zé?"

"She is dead to me. The day she left a fourteen-year-old to be the sole caregiver and provider for an eleven-year-old is the day that she died. The day she let her side nigga chop my daddy's head off in front of me is the day I stopped classifying that woman as my mother. She can rot in hell for all I care. You should warn your father before it's too late for him."

"Hmpp. There is no point trying to tell that man a damn thing. No one tells Chief Carter what to do. He's an asshole," I added.

"What the fuck did you just say?" Alizé said while staring daggers at me before turning to Knight. "Chief Carter is your dad?" she said, shocking the hell out of me with the sudden darkness that appeared in her eyes. The usual beautiful shade of light brown with flecks of green had been replaced by a cold, dark color.

"Yes, how do you know him?" my son asked skeptically

"You bitch!" she screamed as she launched herself at me. Alizé got me one good time in the eye before Knight grabbed hold of her.

"What the fuck are you doing, Zé? That's my damn ma. You can't be trying to get her like that. Sit the fuck back down and tell me what the fuck is going on," Knight ordered, still trying to hold her back.

"It's her fucking fault my daddy is dead. Your dad killed him and took his fucking head home to her!" she screamed.

"These sick motherfuckers were having an affair to get back at my mom and your dad for fucking around, and my dad ended up dead behind it. Let me get the fuck out of here! I can't stay here!" she sobbed while trying to stand up.

Alizé was visibly in a lot of physical and emotional pain thanks to Knight's snooping around.

"Is this shit true, ma?" Knight asked me.

"Yeah, it's true! I saw that man's head."

Turning around, I saw my youngest son and biggest secret, Supreme.

"I'll never forget that night. I was watching a film with ma when pops came back looking mad as fuck. He had been drinking and was carrying this bag around with him. He threw it at her, telling her it was a present for her and when she opened it, she pulled out this head and screamed. She cried for days after that. She kept hugging me and telling me she was sorry. That was right before she left and moved into that house in the suburbs," Supreme disclosed with an attitude.

"What kind of sick motherfucker does something like that?" Alizé screamed.

"Chief is who! Let me just explain," I pleaded. "Please."

"The Chinese food is here... Damn, who died?" Affinity said as she walked out of the house.

"Let's go inside and talk properly, and I promise to tell y'all everything," I urged.

We got inside, and all sat around the dining table. Knight shared the food, and we said grace. Before I began, Alizé spoke.

"Affi and Emi, Knight has found out some things today, which have led to many secrets being exposed. Neither of you girls is babies anymore, but what you are about to hear will upset you both. Just remember that Knight and I love you both very much. Go on, Ava," she finished.

"Both of you boys know what Chief is like. He's not an easy man to live with, but I loved him in the beginning. I knew of him and Serena's affair just two months after Knight's second birthday. We were good friends before we had kids. Your mother and I used to go to the salon together while Chief and Meek ran the streets. When I found out about the affair, I was devastated. Not only did my heart break for my husband but also for the loss of my friend. Chief promised me that the affair had stopped once I found out, but it didn't.

As the years went on, Chief and I became more distant. One night, on our wedding anniversary, we made plans to try to fix our marriage. I booked us a suite at the Waldorf Astoria and waited in the bar for him. He didn't show up that night. He sent me a message telling me that something had come up and that Meek needed his help. So, you can imagine how angry I was when I turned around and saw Meek in the bar talking to one of their business associates. He came over and brought me a drink. The funny thing is your mom had sent him the exact message about me needing her help. It didn't take a genius to figure out that, yet again, they were fucking around behind our backs. We ended up in the suite drinking and talking until the sun came up. We were both so angry that we decided to stay at the hotel for three days. That was the beginning of our affair. It wasn't long before I found out that I was pregnant with Supreme.

Alizé, me and your daddy were in love. We weren't just fooling around. We were waiting for enough proof to go to the courts and get full custody of all five of you. We bought a house, and we were all going to live there together, Knight, you, Supreme, Affinity, Empathy, Meek, and me. We knew Affinity was Chief's daughter, but Meek didn't care. He loved her. She was his baby, and no one could ever tell him any different. You girls were like twins when you were born, and just looking at you now, it is clear you are related. Alizé, you were your daddy's world, the apple of his eye. The day you came along, you changed that man's life and turned him into the man I fell in love with.

I always knew that Supreme was Meek's son from the moment I found out I was pregnant, and I guess Chief did too, which is why he has always been so distant with you, and I am truly sorry for that. Meek loved you guys, and we planned a life together. I couldn't be here after that. I couldn't bear to be around Chief anymore, so I left. I was heartbroken, and instead of clinging to you kids, I pushed everyone away. I'm so sorry. I didn't know that Serena had left you guys alone until just a few weeks ago. I tried to find you in the system when I found out that she was locked in the mental hospital, but no one had any knowledge of you, so I assumed you were with a family member. I would've taken you in and cared for you both. The older you both get, Alizé and Supreme, you look more like him. You both have those eyes that I love so much."

CHAPTER 16

Knight

After listening to my mom's explanation, Alizé made her excuses and went back upstairs to her bedroom. She didn't eat a single bite of her dinner, so I ordered her favorite comfort food: pizza and a tub of ice cream. I sat back down with the rest of the family and finished eating so she could have a minute to herself.

"How do you feel about what was just said, Affi?" I asked.

"I don't really know. I guess it's cool that you're my big brother and that Emi and I are sisters, but I also feel bad for my daddy. I guess I'm just confused. I never really understood why my mom just left us the way she did."

"Well, now you've got two big brothers and another sister to look out for you," I added, trying to make light of the situation.

When the pizza came, I walked up the stairs and knocked on Alizé's door. At first, she didn't answer, but then I called out.

"Come on, Zé Baby, open the door for me."

I heard her walk toward the door and unlock it. She

must've just gotten into bed and cried. Her eyes were red and puffy.

"It hurts my heart to think about my daddy. There isn't a day that I don't miss him like mad. I just know that my life would be so different if he were still here, and none of this bad shit would've happened to me. I don't want to believe that Affinity isn't my full sister, but I also can't deny how much she and Empathy favor each other. Looking at Supreme, I can see my daddy. I hadn't noticed before just how much he looked like him. He has the same shape head and nose as my daddy, and even his smile is identical."

I sat next to her and pulled her in close to me. I had such high hopes of us being together, but after her finding out that it's my pops' fault that her dad is not here, I doubt that will happen now.

"You know I really care about you, Zé, baby. I'm sorry that what I found out hurt you, but I couldn't keep that shit a secret. You deserve the truth, even if it hurts."

"I know you didn't want to hurt me, but it hurt me. I'm also upset because now I know I can never be with you the way I want to be," she confessed.

"Don't say that, baby. We can still be together," I said, full of hope.

"We can't. I always swore that I would find the man who killed my daddy and make him pay for it with his life. How the fuck can I do that when I'm in love with his son? I have to leave tomorrow. Thank you for everything, but I can't stay here with you."

"I can't let you kill my pops, and I won't let you leave me. We can work through this, baby, I promise. I'm in love with you, and I can't let you go. I swear you will never have to see him."

"How can you say that when we live in his damn house,

Knight? The same house he came into with my daddy's severed head in a fucking bag?"

"Fine, we'll leave. I've got enough money to buy a house. My ma can sign off on the paperwork for us. Just don't leave a nigga. Let me have the chance to make you happy."

"I'm sorry, but I need some time. I found a job, and I start next week. I found an apartment right near work and not far from the school. I won't take Affinity away from you, but I need space to get my mind right from this whole situation."

I was mad as fuck, but I had to respect her decision. I went through all that shit getting rid of her fuck boy ex just for my own parents to be why I didn't get my fucking girl.

Just thinking back to when I killed that old nigga made me happy. You should've seen Hardcore's face when big dick Damian came into the room. He knew he was about to get done the way he'd done my baby girl. I made that nigga beg me to end his damn life, but I left him there alive so Damian could have his fun first. The rest of the crew that stayed behind tore that house to pieces and took anything of value. They packed up Zé and Affi's rooms and emptied that nigga's safe. I gave the dough to Zé Baby and let the crew keep the jewelry and bricks they found. They lit that motherfucker up like it was the Fourth of July. That sick old fucker took two to the dome, and so did that snake ass hoe, Yanni, before being left to be cremated in the crib.

I spent the next three days at Alizé's bedside. I didn't leave her alone for a single minute. I prayed harder than ever for her to be ok and pull through this. I moved her into the crib, and I've got to admit I love coming home and cuddling up with her and just talking shit after running the streets all day. I ain't even got that pussy yet. I was giving her time to make sure she was ready and didn't feel forced like she previously had been. I wanted it to be perfect, and now, listening to her, I was about to lose her for good.

"I can respect that, but I don't like it. I'll only ever be at the end of the phone, ma. Don't trip about working. I've signed you up to do your GED online, and I enrolled you in school. It was meant to be a surprise 'cuz I heard how passionate you were about it when we spoke the other night. I'll pay the rent on your apartment for the first year. If you really want to leave, then I can't stop you. I already bought all your books and shit that you need, and I got you a gift. It's outside in the garage. I'll make sure you're good while you're in school, and if you still don't want me, I'll bow out." I threw the keys to the brand-new BMW on the bed, kissed her one last time, and walked out of the room.

I walked straight down the stairs, grabbed a bottle of Parton off the bar I'd installed and straight out the door. Getting into my Range Rover, I turned my stereo system up as loud as it would go and lit the blunt in the ashtray from earlier. I pressed the start button and sped out of the driveway. I just needed to blow off some smoke before I flipped the fuck out and killed the old man my damn self. The first woman that I could see myself settling down with won't even give me the time of day because of the actions of my fucked-up parents, neither of whom actually give a fuck about my siblings or me. They don't even check on us from one month to the next. Their idea of being a good parent is making monthly bank transfers into their children's accounts and the nanny.

Chief thinks as long as the bills are paid and we get money, he's doing his part. He believes my mother should be at home with us, but she won't come and live in the house until he moves all of his things out. They are so damn childish that it's not even funny. They need to just get a divorce, but he knows that she will take his ass for half of everything, and he's too damn greedy to give her what she is owed. Mrs. A has been more of a mom than our own has ever been. She is the one who is there for us every day. The one who nursed us when we were sick and came to all of our sporting events and parent-teacher evenings.

I was not about to lose Zé Baby, and certainly not for some shit over which I had no fucking control. I knew what I had to do. I had to leave with her. I had some money put away, and I knew I would be able to get more. I just had to see my mom.

* * *

Pulling up to her crib, I grabbed my weed and the bottle of Patron I'd been sipping on and went inside.

"Yo, ma! Ma, where you at?" I hollered when I walked in.

She came walking from the back of the house in her fluffy robe with her headscarf on. "Boy, don't bring your drunk ass in here hollering like you got no sense. What the hell is your problem?"

"Y'all are my problem. I love her, ma, and she wants nothing to do with me because of the past. I don't know what to do, ma. She wants to kill pops to avenge her daddy."

"I want the same thing, which is why I can't be around him. Meek was a good man who never should've died, especially not the way he did. Can you imagine poor lil' ZéZé having to watch that shit happen to him at such an early age?" She answered.

"I can't let her kill pops, but I can't lose her either. What do I do, ma?"

"You and your sister are the only reason I haven't killed that man already. I've been thinking about everything since I left earlier, and I want you all to move in here with me. Meek built this house for us all to live in together, and I want you all here with me. The best bit is that your father doesn't know it even exists. There is a three-bedroom guest house for Mrs. Audrey to live in, and there are seven bedrooms inside the main house. It's time I got back to being the mom I should be and gave that poor woman a break. I couldn't live without her, but she's going to be taking it easy from now on. And I want you to let me speak to ZéZé. I think I might be able to convince her."

"Why do you keep calling her ZéZé ma? It's just Zé."

"ZéZé is what Meek always called her when she was small. Leave it to me, son. Now puff, puff pass nigga, sitting over there hogging the whole damn blunt." She laughed as she came and sat down beside me.

We spent the next few hours smoking blunts and chopping it up. My ma was cool as fuck when she was like this, and it was good to get some motherly advice. I was happy as hell that she was ready to be a mom again. The others needed her, and I needed to be able to get my own crib without worrying about my siblings.

My mom said she would be over at the house first thing in the morning to make sure everyone was there and up early. I hugged her and left. I was part of the way home when I decided that I was going to confront my pops and that hoe Serena, but I was going to wait til Zé was ready. We could face them together and find out the answers she needs to hear. Only then would she be ready to move forward. All I knew was that I would be with her every step of the way. We are meant to be together, and nothing or no one is going to stop us.

CHAPTER 17

Alizé

I felt safe for the first time in forever, and now I had to leave. Knight is everything I could want in a man, and he makes me feel things I never thought I would feel. After everything that happened with Hardcore, I didn't think it was possible to fall in love with someone or even to want them sexually. Knight changed all of that. He had made me want it all. I finally feel like I can imagine a future where I am happy, one where I have a normal family and children and an amazing man next to me.

I didn't want to leave him, and I wish I had said yes when he said he would leave with me, but he'll be a constant reminder of the man who killed my daddy and ruined my life. I took Affi and Emi out with me, and we spent a few hours driving around town in my new car, then I took them shopping and out to eat. I loved it. It felt so good just to be young and carefree. Maybe going back to school won't be so bad. I might even make some friends.

I hate that I had to leave my old friends behind because I get really lonely now. Losing Knight won't be easy. He is the only friend I have right now. I'd come to love him and really look forward to him coming home at night and chilling with me. I know he could be out there with any chick he wants, so I love that he chooses me even though we've not slept together yet. Don't get me wrong. I want to. It's just that I'm too scared to make a move on him, and he's too much of a gentleman to try to fuck me.

Supreme came home, and we smoked a few blunts outside while I answered his questions about our father. I was sad that he never got to know what a great man our dad really was. I always wanted a brother, and I know my dad would've loved him. He told me that he didn't want any parts of the street life, and he planned to go off to school to play basketball. He planned to study business so that way if he didn't get drafted, he would have something to fall back on.

I was excited as hell to be going back to school and couldn't wait for a new challenge. It would be hard as hell studying and working enough to pay the bills and keep this little diva in the life that she has so quickly become accustomed to, but I was down for it.

The thought of that man wanting to get to know Affinity is too much for me to even consider, and I can only pray that she doesn't want to build a relationship with her biological father. I still can't believe that Knight knows where to find my mother. A part of me wants to see her, to ask her the questions I have gone over a million times in my head. A part of me also knows that if I am in close proximity to that man, I will want to kill his ass and quite possibly want to kill my mother too. When I think of all the shit I have had to endure because of her selfish actions, I want to torture her. To simply shoot her wouldn't be enough.

* * *

I was half asleep and as high as a giraffe's pussy when I heard a light knocking at my door in the middle of the night.

"Zé Baby, let me in." I got out of bed and walked over to the door. Pulling it open, Knight was there looking drunk and high. His eyes were so low that I could barely see them.

"I can't lose you," he said as he walked into my room.

Picking me up, he wrapped my legs around him and kissed me hard. As Knight backed me into the wall, he stopped to look at me. "I love you, Alizé, and I won't let some shit that our parents did affect us being happy. We're meant to be together. Fate brought you into my life, and I'm not letting you go."

"I love you too, Knight," I expressed as I kissed him back. It was the most intense kiss I had ever felt. I was in love with this man, and I never wanted to let him go.

Walking us over to my bed, Knight laid me on my back and stood up to take his shirt off. I looked at his body as he leaned down to kiss me again. This time when he pulled back, he lifted my shirt from over my head and pulled my shorts off of me. "I need you, Zé Baby. I need to feel you."

He was so gentle with me, but I could feel the urgency in his touch. "Are you ok? Do you want me to stop?"

"No, don't stop. I want you, Knight," I replied.

He slowly peeled off his clothes and pushed my legs back. He dove into my kitty headfirst, and I thought I had died and gone to heaven. I'd never felt pleasure like this in my life, but then again, I had never had sex and wanted it before, either. If it felt like this, I knew I had been missing out.

Slowly, Knight pushed himself into me inch by inch until he was fully in. He was so big I felt like he would split me in half. Knight slowly started moving in and out of me, and his stroke game was official. He was so gentle, kissing me and looking into my eyes as he made love to my body and mind. The way he had me feeling was like I was in heaven. He had me shaking and cumming in minutes. I had never experienced such intense orgasms before Knight, and I knew that I was going to be hooked from this point on. I needed this man like I needed air. He was like a drug to me, and I would do anything for this feeling to never end.

After making love for another hour, we lay back on my bed in each other's arms. This was the most perfect moment of my life, and I wanted nothing to ruin it. I finally felt at peace. I was just upset that this wouldn't last. I still planned to leave as soon as possible, but it would be more complicated now that we had finally slept with each other.

It's like Knight read my mind.

"You're not leaving me, Zé Baby. We're going to find a way to be together. If I have to leave everything and come with you, I will. I love you, and I never thought it possible to find someone who gets me the way you do. You just got to stop trying to fight it. Trust that your man has got you. I promise I'll never let anyone hurt you again."

That was the last thing I remember until I woke up to the sound of someone knocking on the bedroom door.

"Wakey, wakey, everyone," the voice on the other side said as I heard knocking further down the hall. I got up and pulled my robe around me. I peeped my head out of the door to see Ms. Ava standing there talking to Emi and Affi. When she noticed me, she turned around and walked back toward where I was standing.

"Morning ZéZé, I would like to take you for breakfast. Just the two of us, so we can talk. I'll wait for you downstairs"

"Erm, ok, sure. Just give me thirty minutes to get ready," I replied.

Knight was sitting up in the bed, looking at his phone when I walked back into the room.

"Why does your mom want to take me to breakfast, Knight?" I asked.

"She wants to talk to you about an idea we've had," he answered, without taking his eyes off the screen.

I went into the bathroom to shower. Just as I finished washing my body Knight walked in, and he just stood there looking at me.

"You getting in?" I asked with a huge smile on my face.

"Baby, if I get in there, you will never make it out of this house. Plus, my ma ain't got no filter, so if you're taking too long, her ass will be up in here chasing you out. We got a busy ass day ahead of us, so I'm gone get ready myself, and I'll see you when you get back. Then we can have that steamy ass shower you want. I'ma turn you into a little freak, just watch."

"I never knew it could feel so good, and that's a feeling I never want to end," I admitted shyly. He walked over to me and kissed me before replying.

"I ain't ever had sex with a chick I loved before, so that was special to me too, baby. Normally, I just fuck for the sake of fucking. With you, I needed you, and as soon as I got inside you, I knew this was where I wanted to be for the rest of my life. Promise me you'll listen to what she says to you and have an open mind."

"I promise, and I love you too," I said, kissing him again.

* * *

Half an hour later, I was heading down the stairs to meet Ms. Ava. We got into the car and drove to a nice little breakfast spot she knew. We both ordered our food and made small talk until the server placed the food in front of us. I prepared myself for what she could have to say.

"I should never have tried to hit you. I'm sorry," I started.

"Don't be sorry. I would've done the same thing. I want you to know that I really did love Meek, and I still do. I never knew that Chief would react the way he did, and if I had, I never would have put your daddy in that position. I told y'all that your father and I had bought a house, so we could all be together. Well, I haven't been there since he was killed. The memories were just too painful, but I drove there and went inside after leaving y'all the other day. I was like I could feel his energy all around the place. We had just finished refurbishing and decorating it the way he wanted it.

The day your father died, he was in the house, and he sent me a message telling me about a surprise. What I never knew was that he had gotten a designer to paint a picture on the wall of the seven of us; Him, me, you, Knight, Supreme, Affinity and Empathy. It was supposed to be our fresh start.

The second I found out what happened with your mother I looked for you and your sister. I wanted to make sure you were ok, but I couldn't find you. I believe in fate, and I believe that our loved ones are guiding us from heaven. If I weren't so caught up in my own grief, then I would've known straight away who you were, so I am sorry for that.

Our love for your daddy is not the only thing we have in common. We both love my son, and last night he came to me and asked me what he could do to stop you from leaving him. I understand that you don't want to be with him because of Chief, but please don't make my baby pay for his father's fucked up ways. Knight is nothing like Chief, and he'll do anything to protect you. He would never hurt you or allow anyone else to. I've never seen Knight like this about a female. That boy is so in love with you. Just give him the chance to show you that."

I took in everything Ava said, and I believed that she really did love my daddy.

"I would like to see the painting if you don't mind. I only have a few pictures of my daddy left. And yes, I do love your son very much, but I can't be with Knight, knowing that I want to kill his father. How can we have a relationship with any chance of a future? I could never be around that man or let my future children even know him, which is not fair to

Knight. I feel that I would have to compromise my feelings about my daddy for the man that I love, and I can't do that."

"Well, that brings me to why I wanted to see you alone today. I want us all to move into the house your daddy and I built. Chief doesn't know it even exists, and neither does your mother. It is what your daddy wanted and what he would want me to do now. There is no way that I can let you continue to be alone in this world, and you're too young to be Affi's mom. You need to let someone else be the responsible one and enjoy your life. You've sacrificed so much these last few years, and it's time to do you now ZéZé. Let me take the reins and look after you and Affinity now. Go back to school, make some friends, and enjoy what's left of your teenage years. I can promise you that Chief will not be around much longer, and you'll never have to see him," she said with a wink.

"What do you mean he won't be around much longer?" I asked.

"What I am about to tell you stays between us. You can never repeat this to Knight or anyone. Since the day he killed Meek, I've wanted to kill Chief's ass," she whispered, "but I had to wait until Knight was old enough. You see, during our marriage, Chief has built a very lucrative empire, and if Knight is over the age of eighteen when he dies, then everything will be left to Knight. If Chief were to die before then, his brother, Major, would get to take over. He ruined my life, but I couldn't ruin my sons. Leading this empire is Knight's birthright, and I won't let anyone take what's his."

I didn't know what to say. For a second, I just sat stunned, trying to process what Ava was saying.

"Let's continue this conversation in the car. I'll take you to see the house," she said as she stood up and put a fifty-dollar bill on the table.

"Ok," was all I could manage as I got up and walked to the car with her.

I can't believe this woman just sat there and told me she planned on killing her husband. If he were out of the way, then I maybe wouldn't feel the need to leave Knight, and although I wanted my own place, I would still be able to see him.

CHAPTER 18

Ava

After finishing my breakfast with ZéZé, we headed over to the house.

"Your daddy designed the house himself. We chose every single aspect of it ourselves with you kids in mind. It was supposed to be our perfect fresh start, but that bastard Chief ruined it all," I spoke. I could feel myself getting upset, so I stopped to compose myself.

"What were you saying back there before we finished our food?" she asked me. I was dubious about sharing my secret with anyone, but I had to convince her to stay.

"Can I trust you with something important? You can't tell anyone, not even Knight." I asked, and Alizé shook her head yes.

"So, Knight is going to be eighteen in a few weeks. Once that has happened, there is no reason for that man to be left alive. He's only made it this far because of my plan for Knight's future. The power, status, and money are the only reason I have left Chief alive after he killed your dad, which was all I had left to cling to."

"So, you're planning to..." Alizé looked around before finishing her sentence. "You know, kill him?"

"Yes, but you can't tell a soul. It would break Knight's heart to know of my plan. He can never know. None of them can ever know. You know the old saying is true. What they don't know can't hurt them. Can I trust you, ZéZé?" I asked.

"No one has called me that since my daddy was alive."

"I'm sorry."

"No, don't be. You can call me that. I don't mind. You really did love him, didn't you?"

"Yes, very much so. Meek was and still is the love of my life," I answered honestly. I opened the one of the huge double entrance doors and ushered ZéZé to walk in before me.

The second you walked into the house, there it was, the masterpiece. In the foyer hung a huge painting of Meek, me, and all five of our children. The look on ZéZé's face was priceless.

"It's beautiful. The whole thing looks like a photograph."

"Do you want me to show you your room? Well, the room Meek picked out for you. He had it all planned. We chose each of your rooms before...."

"I would like that. If feels a bit weird seeing us all there in the picture and knowing this is what he wanted in his last days."

"It's fate that you and Knight met each other. You were always meant to be in each other's lives. Don't let Chief ruin that for you. When you find love that pure you have to hold on to it. Come on, let's go upstairs."

As we walked around the house, I showed her all the rooms and where we had planned on each of them being.

"I want us to live here together, ZéZé. I promise to protect you and make sure that you are never hurt like that again. Please let me do this. Knight told me about you getting your GED so you can go back to school, and I'm proud of you, as would your daddy be. You have overcome so much, too much. The things you have endured are truly awful and it's enough to have broken the strongest of women. Just know that these trials will mold you into one hell of a woman. You are amazing, and you've done so well with Affi on your own. Just let someone else look after you both for a change. Leave the boring mom stuff to me and go out there and be a teenager. I hate to pull this card on you, but you know your daddy would want you to enjoy your life knowing that Affi is being taken care of," I said, repeating what I'd told her over breakfast.

"I don't know what to say. Thank you for your offer, but —" she started, but I cut her off before she rejected the idea altogether.

"Please just give it a few months, and if you don't like it, I'll buy you your very own house."

"I was going to say I have to ask Affi first, but I would like that. If I'm honest, I'm tired of dealing with everything on my own, and it's like I can feel my daddy here. I can see him every day with that huge ass picture down there."

"I'm so happy that you agreed. They have just pulled up with the truck. That could've been awkward."

We both shared a laugh as the front door opened. In walked Knight, looking like the boss that he is and Mrs. Audrey, followed by Supreme, Emi, and Affi. Everyone stopped to look at the painting on the wall.

"Shit, that's my pops? I look hella like that nigga!" Supreme noted while everyone agreed.

"Let me show you all to your rooms," I said, leaving Knight and ZéZé alone to talk.

Alizé's room was opposite ours. Emi and Affi's rooms were along the hall from us, and their rooms were joined with a shared bathroom in the middle. We must've known that they would be the best of friends. Supreme and Knight's rooms were at the other end of the long hall, as we didn't want the three teenagers together. Lord knows what kind of problems they would've given us over the years in this house. I was happy that our dream house would finally be filled with our kids just like we always wanted, even if my Meek wasn't here to see it.

There were memories of Meek everywhere in this house, and the picture in the foyer was the icing on the cake. I couldn't wait to make more memories here with our children. Finally, I feel like the future might not be as bleak as I had once thought. Now I just had to finalize my plan on how to kill Chief and not get caught.

I knew his routine. Chief was getting too cocky. He thought he could never be touched, but I would show him that even bosses can get touched. The best part of it is that I could get real close without him suspecting anything. He won't think that I have it in me to actually hurt him. He thinks it's because I'm weak, and I still love him despite everything he has done to me over the years. Over the years, I have threatened to kill him or even divorce him a million times but never followed through on my plan.

What Chief doesn't know is that after he killed Meek, any love I had for him was dead. I was void of any emotion when it came to him. The only thing I have left is my kids, and I'll be damned if I was going to lose all our money as well as my mind. I know that if I stay married to Chief, he will continue to make monthly deposits into my account and keep all of my bills paid.

As soon as Knight hit's eighteen years old, everything Chief owns will be left to my son. He has been primed for this his entire life, and he is more than ready to take over from his father. I wouldn't do anything to risk that happening, which is why I need to get rid of him before he finds out that Knight is with Alizé. That bitch Serena better not even try to come for these girls now because she will not win. She should've learned not to fuck with me.

The last time I wanted to hurt her, I had her hooked-on heroin, but that bastard Chief still took her back. If it's the last thing I ever do, I will ensure they don't get their happily ever after. They took mine from me with Meek so they can go fuck themselves. I might just leave her alive for now, but that is only so she can feel what it is like to live without the man you love, just like I have since Chief killed Meek. I would love to make my darling husband suffer or even suffer the same fate he delivered to Meek but seeing him in his casket would be enough for me. I have gone over this repeatedly in my head, and I have at least ten ways that I would like to kill him. Luckily for him, he can only die once.

CHAPTER 19

Knight

As soon as Alizé left with my ma this morning, I sent the girls to pack up all of her shit from her room. The movers turned up and had all our shit loaded onto the truck within an hour. Mrs. A packed up and was ready after receiving a call from my mom last night.

We piled into my car and headed to the new crib. It was about thirty minutes away and in the opposite direction of the condo my pops stayed in. All the way there, I was praying that my ma managed to talk Zé into staying. I wasn't letting her leave me before, and I damn sure ain't letting her leave me now, especially not after last night. I'm going to look stupid as a motherfucker if she says no. If all else fails, I'll just pay for a suite for a month, and my ma can sign off on a crib for her. I can't wait to be eighteen, so I'll be able to do what the fuck I want and won't have to ask for anyone's help.

With the moves I've been making in the streets, I'll have the money for a mini mansion in no time. That plus all the money my pops has been depositing in our accounts, we're all pretty much set for life, and now I need to make sure Affi gets the same. I know Zé ain't gone want a cent of his money, but that's fine 'cuz I plan to make enough money for both of us to never have to lift a finger for the rest of our lives unless we want to.

After we are settled in, I need to take Zé to get the answers she deserves from her mother. I, on the other hand, needed to know why my pops was so damn heartless. I know that being a boss entails more than you might think, and I understand that when the time comes, we all have to get our hands dirty, but there was a code we lived by, which was never to involve innocent people. Kids were off limits, and what he did was cowardly and evil. If he and Meek had a beef, it should've been dealt with in the streets. My pops was dead ass wrong for what he did, especially when you find out that he killed him for having an affair with my mom when he himself had been having an affair with that man's wife for years. They were all some fucked up individuals in a fucked-up situation, but I'll be damned if I let them fuck up my chances at being happy with Zé Baby.

Once I pulled up in the driveway of my mom's crib, I said another quick prayer and got out of the car. Walking into the house, I saw my mom and Zé Baby standing in front of a huge ass picture that was painted on the wall. Just looking at it, I knew it had to be Zé Baby's pops. Looking at him is like looking at an older version of Reme. No wonder my pops is always distant with Supreme. Don't get me wrong. He looks out for Reme the same as he does with Emi and me. He gives him an allowance and shit like that, but they don't really fuck with each other too tough.

Being as subtle as she always is, my mom took the others to show them their rooms and left me alone with Zé.

"So, you down? You gone stay with your nigga or nah?" I asked while holding onto her hips.

"Yeah, I'ma stay with you. I think me and your mom will get along fine, and Affi is happy too, which is the main thing."

"No, baby, you being ok is the main thing. Affi will always be fine. We can still take this as slow as you want. I'm just happy you're staying. All the way here, I was praying that you would be ok with this 'cuz all of your shit is in the truck out front."

"Ohh, I see you. What made you so sure I would say yes?"

"Nah, I wasn't sure of shit. Look, I even brought out enough bread to pay for you to have a suite 'til my mom signed your lease," I told her, pulling a roll of money out of my pocket. We both shared a laugh, but I was hella serious. I pulled Zé in close and kissed her. It felt a bit weird with a huge ass painting of her pops staring at us, but I needed to feel her kiss right now.

* * *

The rest of the evening was spent with all of us getting settled into our new bedrooms. I didn't want to push it and put my stuff with Zé but ain't no way baby girl wasn't gone be in bed with me every damn night. Once everything was situated, I made my way to the kitchen to see what my beautiful lady was cooking for dinner tonight, but I was shocked to see my mom in the kitchen frosting a damn cake. I had to laugh 'cuz I can't remember her ever baking shit since I was a kid.

"Hey ma, where's Mrs. A? She ain't gone like you being in her kitchen," I half joked.

"I don't know why you over there laughing. Boy, this is my kitchen. Your mama can cook now, remember? I can throw it down in here when I'm ready. On a serious note, though, you were right. Mrs. Audrey does too much, so I have given her the night off, but she will join us at eight o'clock for dinner. She's over in the guest house at the moment, choosing her color scheme and furniture. I gave her the black card and told her to choose anything she wanted.

We can donate the furniture that she doesn't want to the shelter."

"Thanks, ma. I don't know what you and Zé Baby discussed today, but she's a lot happier here. I think that huge ass shrine to her pops might've helped, but however you did it, you still did it, so thank you."

"I've let you all down, and for that, I am sorry. I let my grief take over, and it clouded my judgment. I'm happy that I have a chance to make it all right again and look after ZéZé and Affi just like Meek would want me to."

* * *

Over the next few weeks, Alizé got settled into her studies. She was so clever, and I'm glad that she has done this for herself. She was getting on great with Supreme, and I would often get home to see them sitting in the chairs in front of the painting of us all, talking about their dad. A lot of the time, my mom would be there with them, reminiscing. It's a whole part of her life that none of us knew about, so it's good that she doesn't have to hide that anymore.

This street shit was going crazy right now. There was a war between two of the gangs, which led to a lot of deaths and a lot of arrests, clearing the path for me to take over. We've seized the opportunity to open new traps and expand our operation into new territory. My pops is still my plug, and business is booming. I've also been having meetings about supplying some cats from Tennessee whose plug got knocked off a few months back. They seem serious and have the cash to front ten bricks. I don't really like to fuck with new niggas, but I've had the private investigator look into them, and they seem legit. If I could start supplying a few more of these types, I would be raking it in even more than I am now. Unlike my pops, I don't want to be in the game when I'm an old man. I plan to make my money, stack that shit, and get out of the game before I'm thirty. By then, I'll be fully legit and own a few businesses. This street life ain't for the old man. You gotta get that shit while you young and get out while you still can.

Tomorrow is the night of my eighteenth birthday, and I can't wait to party hard. We were having a family dinner followed by a party at the club. Today I'ma take my baby shopping and making sure we're looking fly for the occasion. As I pulled up to the crib, I grabbed my phone and went inside in search of Zé Baby. I found her in the kitchen talking to my mom. They were both still cut up about this nigga Meek, so it's good that they finally had someone to talk to about him. I still can't get over my pops going after that man when he was doing the same thing. I guess it really is one rule for him and one for everyone else. He's lucky my ma ain't just flipped the fuck out and killed that bitch Serena just to get back at him.

We walked around the mall hand in hand, going in and out of stores looking for the perfect outfits. Zé was being real quiet and wouldn't tell me what was going on. She wanted to look in stores that I wouldn't usually go to, the cheaper, more budget stores. I couldn't believe it when she tried to pay for her own shit at the register. I just looked at her as I handed the woman behind the register a load of hundred-dollar bills. When we got outside, I spoke on it.

"Is this why you ain't wanted to look at shit in the Gucci or Chanel stores?"

"Knight, this is all the money I have, and I want to look good for you tomorrow, but I can't just throw away money on such high-priced pieces. I'm sorry. I knew I should've just come on my own."

"I never want you to worry about money again. I've got you. You're my woman. It's my job to make the money and your job to spend that shit making yourself happy. You can have the world, baby. Don't ever think that you can't spend what the hell you want to spend. Shit, if you keep hanging around my OG, I'll be bankrupt in a few months, anyway. I'm happy that you both have each other to talk to while I'm out in the streets working."

"Thank you, baby, but it's my job as your woman to look after you. Not spend all the money you out there making. Your mom has been real good to me, and I love how she loved my daddy. When she talks about him, her eyes light up. You can tell that their love was true. I hate my mother even more now than I did before, but I want answers from her Knight. I need to know why she did the things she did and how she could just leave us and not come back?"

"Do you want to see her? I know where she is, and we can stop by there if you want to. My pops is out of town until tomorrow, so you won't have to see him."

"Ok, if you're sure he won't be there."

"I'm sure, but first, get your ass in that store and find the most expensive ass dress, shoes, and purse you can find, and meet me over at the food court. I've got a couple of phone calls to make," I instructed her before kissing her and handing her my card to pay for anything she wanted.

CHAPTER 20

Alizé

As we pulled up to the building that my ma lived in with that snake bastard Chief, I was nervous as hell and didn't want to lose it in front of her. I wanted to remain calm and get the answers that I needed so I could close the door on that part of my life once and for all.

"You ok, baby?" Knight asked as he held my hand in the elevator.

"I will be. I just need to hear her out, and then we can leave and go home."

Knight knocked on the door, and a minute later, the door was opened. There she was — my mother.

"Oh my god, Alizé baby, is that you? I'm so happy that you're here. I just knew I would see you again," she said as she pulled the door open wider for us to enter.

"Yes, it's me, but this isn't a social visit. I just need some answers."

We went in and sat down while she sat in the chair opposite us. Looking around, it was clear that she had landed on her feet. This place was huge and looked like it came straight out of a magazine. She just kept staring at me and wiping away the crocodile tears that were falling.

"I'm so happy to see you, baby girl. I've missed you and your sister so much. I tried so hard to find you once they let me out of the hospital, but you'd moved out of the house. You see, the day I left, I went out to get some food for you and your sister, and I had a complete breakdown in the store. They called the hospital, and I was detained under the mental health act. I was kept there for six months, but I was too scared to tell them about you both as I feared that you would be taken into CPS custody, and I would never see either of you again. When I got out, I came straight home, but neither of you was there. I stayed there for a few weeks, hoping you would come home, but you never did. I even asked the neighbors, but no one had seen either of you for months."

"You didn't come back after six months, cuz I held shit down there for longer than that. Did you even try to find us?" I asked, as it actually dawned on me how she didn't even come looking for us.

"I swear I did. I wanted to find you both."

"If you really wanted to find us, why are you in Chicago?" I questioned.

"I heard that you were here from Mrs. Jones next door, so I came here looking for you."

"The funny thing is, we didn't tell anyone where we were going. Affi didn't even know until we were leaving to get the bus, so I know that you're lying. How the fuck could you leave us like we weren't shit to you? Clearly, all you cared about was that bastard man who killed my daddy, got you hooked on drugs, and ruined my childhood. Oh, and let's not forget, he's the same man who fathered my fucking sister! You led my daddy to believe she was his daughter, but the whole time she belonged to your side nigga! Well, the joke is on you, 'cuz neither of you will ever know that girl."

"Please, Alizé! It's not my fault. I had no control over what happened."

I have a hundred questions running around in my head, but after speaking with her for a while, I can see that she hasn't changed one bit. She can't take responsibility for her actions and keeps placing the blame on everyone but herself. After being there for just twenty minutes, I could see that this was a pointless exercise. She would never think she did anything wrong, and I was already sick of the sound of her voice.

"You know something, Serena? You are to blame for all of this. You didn't fucking look for me. If your hot pussy self weren't out cheating, then my dad would be alive. It's hardly surprising that he chose Ava over you. She is everything that you're not. She is intelligent, caring, loving and beautiful. You're nothing but a selfish, cheating, lying bitch. You only care about yourself and that bastard Chief. Did you once stop and think about what you did to my sister and me? Because of you, I was raped, beaten, and forced to sleep with men for money. I almost died at the hands of a man twice my age 'cuz I had no other choice.

If Knight hadn't saved us when he did, they would've done the same thing to Affinity. But did you care? No, you were too busy playing house with the man who killed my daddy. I swear I will make you regret the day you said fuck your family. Come on, Knight, let's get out of here."

As I stood to leave, she begged me to see her again and bring Affi. I didn't make any promises 'cuz I knew that I wouldn't be coming back here again, and I knew that if I had my way, she would be joining her nigga in hell sooner rather than later.

The second I got into the car and closed the door, the tears started to fall. She wasn't even sorry. It is her fault that my daddy is dead, and I'll never forgive her for leaving us to fend for ourselves. It had me asking if the plan to kill Chief could also include that snake bitch he lays with? I wanted to make her hurt the way I was hurt. I lost my childhood, innocence, virginity, and almost my life behind her unfit ass, and I want her to pay for it. I knew without a shadow of a doubt that I would get my revenge on the both of them motherfuckers.

* * *

The second I got in the house, I went looking for Ava while Knight was still in the car, taking a business call. I knocked on her bedroom door, and she called out for me to enter.

"We went to see her," I relayed as I sat down on her bed.

"Who do you mean, baby? Serena?"

"Yes. I swear, Ava, I'm going to hurt her. I want in on the plan. I want to help you."

"Are you sure? She is your mom at the end of the day, ZéZé. I want you to think about it, and we'll discuss it after Knight's birthday. If you decide it is what you really want, then fine. We'll do it, but only after he has been gone a few weeks. She needs to feel the pain of losing the man she loves just like I did, and then we'll take her out of her misery."

I got up and hugged her just as Knight walked into the room. She held me a few seconds longer before pulling back and kissing my cheek.

"You'll be ok, ZéZé. You've got us. You don't need her, and you never have to see her again if you don't want to."

"Thank you."

"My mom's right, baby girl. You ain't ever got to go back there again," Knight said. "Anyway, go and try these dresses on and show ma what you got. I've got a few calls to make and a couple of runs, but then I'm yours for the rest of the night." He put the bags down and kissed me before leaving the room and closing the door behind him.

I turned back to Ava. "Did a delivery come for me today?"

"Yes, Mrs. Audrey left it in your room."

"It's Knight's birthday gift. I'm a bit nervous about his party, though. I've never been in a club before, and I'm not even old enough. What if they don't let me in? I'll be so embarrassed in front of his friends."

"You'll be fine. No one would dare ask you for ID when you're with Knight. You really don't know how much weight my son's name holds in the streets yet, do you? You will learn soon, sweetie. Knight will be an even bigger name when he takes over the running of the day-to-day operations. The Carters are one of the biggest families in the entire state, ZéZé. Now don't get me wrong, I love that you love my son purely for him and not for the money, cars, and jewelry like his previous girlfriends, but you'll have to get used to his status. It will mean a lot of late nights spent awake worrying, there will be women throwing themselves at him and no doubt a few other issues along the way, but with me, by your side, I will mold you into the boss bitch that you were born to be. Tomorrow will be the first time he is showing you off, so it is necessary that you look the part. I have booked an entire day of pampering for us, Mrs. Audrey, Affi, and Emi."

"Thank you so much, Ava. I really don't know what I would do without you, and I don't doubt that with your help, I can be everything Knight needs me to be."

The rest of the evening was spent at home, catching up on my studies while waiting for Knight to return. I was looking forward to a day of pampering tomorrow. I've been thinking about getting a weave. I saw some really hot styles with some long ass hair which I think would suit me. I couldn't wait until Knight's birthday. I got him a new Rolex, which I had engraved with the date we first met and our initials. I didn't really know what to get him, but Supreme helped me with the idea.

CHAPTER 21

Knight

The day I've been waiting for was here at last. Your boy is finally eighteen. When I woke up this morning, the sun was shining, and I had the girl of my dreams next to me. My mom had us up early as hell, so we could eat the huge ass breakfast that she and Mrs. A had whipped up. We sat around the table eating, and for the first time in years, it felt like I had a normal family. Everyone handed me their gifts, and I loved each of them, but my favorite was my new Rolex from Zé Baby for sure.

My pops sent me a message asking me to meet him for lunch and to bring my sisters. I knew for sure that Zé wouldn't go for that, so it's just as well that they had plans already, and I wouldn't have to lie to him. He doesn't tolerate disrespect in the slightest, so to lie to him is out of the question. I don't know how I'll manage to keep these two apart, but I'll find a way. I promised her that she would never have to see him, and I had every intention of keeping that promise to my woman. I was not prepared to lose her for anything, not even my pops.

While the ladies were all out at the salon, I would collect the dough from the traps. Deliveries would be made in the morning 'cuz the whole operation was shut down for the night to honor your boy. It wasn't every day that the boss in line was celebrating a big birthday, so it was only fitting that the entire Legion was out to show their love. It would be the first time that Zé Baby met them all properly if you don't count Sway's bachelor party and all my niggas knew not to even mention that shit to anyone.

* * *

We all sat around the table in the restaurant, enjoying a meal before the party. A few of my closest associates were there with their girlfriends, my mom, siblings, and of course, my Zé. When she stepped out tonight, she was looking fly as fuck, and I couldn't wait to get in them guts later. She got her hair done earlier and came home looking like at least twenty-one with the butt-length weave, long ass nails, and makeup on. Zé was beautiful before, but tonight she was guaranteed to be one of the baddest in the club, and she was all mine.

I heard his voice before I saw him. I just knew that I shouldn't have told his ass where the dinner was being held. I explained over lunch earlier that my mom would be there, and I didn't want anything to ruin the night. In all honesty, I didn't want him fucking up the mood and upsetting Zé.

"Son, I couldn't miss your birthday dinner. I'm sorry I'm late. Your mom forgot to let me know the time," my pops said as he swanned in, wearing his trademark suit and trench coat.

"Pops, I thought we spoke about this earlier?" I asked as I felt Zé Baby tense up next to me. I grabbed her hand under the table to reassure her.

"We did, but I couldn't pass up the opportunity to finally come and meet my new daughter," he said while pulling out a seat for Serena to sit down and then taking the seat next to her. He looked over at my mom. "Hello, my darling wife."

"Mommy?" Affi asked, looking like she was about to cry.

"Husband dear, I didn't realize you were bringing a whore to dinner. You should've said something. I would've asked them if heroin was on the menu. After all, that is her favorite."

"Fuck you, Ava. You think you're so high and mighty, sitting here with my children playing mommy when you've hardly bothered with your own for the last few years," Serena spoke up until my pops looked at her, and she quickly shut up.

"Speaking of bringing whores to dinner..." he continued. "I see you've found yourself a whore to bring to dinner too, son. I hope this is not the girl you were telling me about. I will not let you be with *her*. Did she tell you how for a hundred dollars, you can do whatever you want to her? That is still the going rate isn't it, sweetheart? At least it was when Hardcore owned her. You don't want her son. She's used goods. This one has been 'round the whole damn city. Lord knows what nasty diseases she's got. I hope you haven't fucked her raw," he sneered.

I turned to Alizé, who by now had a tear-stained face as she sat there staring at my father.

"You... You..." she stuttered.

"Chief, get out. I want you to leave now!" my mom demanded. "How dare you come in here and start this bullshit on your son's birthday? Can't you see you're upsetting the girls?" Looking at my little sisters, they were linked arms and huddled in close with tears in their eyes.

"He needed to know the truth about his girlfriend. If you continue this relationship, I will have no option but to disown you. You will not make a dollar in my city while you're with this slut. Did she tell you she fucked me?"

"You raped me, you sick motherfucker! You watched him inject me with drugs, and you raped me! Did you know who I was then? Is that why you did it? And all this time, you were fucking my mom? You're sick!" Alizé spewed.

"Yo, what the fuck, man? Pops. are you for real?" I asked. Now I was hot as hell. Standing up, I flipped the whole fucking table. How the fuck did this nigga just walk up in here to tell me he was one of the sick bastards who took advantage of my damn girl?

"GET THE FUCK OUT!" I turned around to see my mom had upped her strap and had it aimed at my pops. "I'm not fucking playing with you, Chief! Get the fuck out before I put a hole in you and that whore! You are one sick individual. This poor child was pimped out and drugged because her whore of a mother was too dick hungry to leave you or that damn needle alone. You ruined my life, and you ruined theirs all because you were jealous! Meek was a hundred times the man that you are!" She grabbed Zé and held her close. "Both of you get out now! You got three seconds before I shoot, and my aim is on point, nigga. you taught me well."

In all my life, I had never seen my mom boss up like she just did. I would be proud of her if I weren't still reeling from the revelation that my pops fucked my chick.

* * *

We made our way outside of the restaurant to head to the club, but I wasn't in the mood to party. Alizé tried to speak to me, but I couldn't right now. She was still crying, and my mom and sisters were all surrounding her, hugging her. Even my damn brother just shook his head at me like this was my fault somehow.

"You boys go on to the club and have a good night. I'm going to take the girls home," my mom said. As she hugged me, she whispered in my ear. "Boy, you're lucky it's your birthday, or I would slap the black off you. You know what that poor child went through at the hands of that man. You will not blame her for what happened to her. Yes, I understand that what he just said made you feel some type of way, but you will not shame her for what happened to her. She is the victim. If you don't fix this shit before you leave, then you're no better than him."

I took Alizé's hand and walked to the car. When we got inside, I looked over at her beautiful face and instantly felt like an asshole. Her makeup was ruined. She had black streaks down her face from her mascara running when she was crying and smudge marks from where she wiped her tears.

"I'm sorry, baby. It's not your fault. None of what happened was your fault. It just fucked my head up to hear that. I shouldn't have flipped out, but he got me so heated. Do you forgive me?"

"Of course I do. I love you. I'm not going to come out tonight now, though. I can't meet all of your friends looking like this. I look a mess. I'm just going to go home and get into bed. I hope you understand. Enjoy the rest of your birthday, Knight." Alizé leaned over and kissed my jaw before she opened the door and called out to my mom to wait for her. I sat there for a minute trying to gather my thoughts before pulling off. Her lips may have said she'll forgive me, but her eyes told me a different story. I already know, this is going to take more than an apology to fix.

* * *

The club was packed to capacity, and the party was lit as fuck. I grabbed myself a bottle and sat my ass down in the VIP section. I wasn't in the mood for partying now, but it was my damn birthday, and I had to be here. The entire Legion was here to celebrate your boy, and I was trying to enjoy myself.

As I sat drinking the bottle and watching the crowd, I didn't notice the figure sitting down beside me until she spoke.

"Happy birthday, baby, I've missed you," Nat said, as she leaned forward and kissed my jaw.

"Hey Nat, thanks for coming. Who are you here with?" I asked, not really caring about her answer.

"It's just me tonight. I was hoping to catch you alone. I've been trying to reach out, but you blocked me. I hate to have to show up to your birthday, but I need you to know that I'm pregnant and you're the dad. Happy birthday."

"Nat, I never spilled my seeds in you, so try that shit with a next nigga. You and I both know that baby ain't mine."

"That night you were drunk, remember?"

"Holla at me when it's time for a DNA test," I stated as I got up, leaving her looking stupid. It is just as well my fucking chick ain't come tonight to hear that shit. She would be leaving me for damn sure after hearing that shit.

* * *

I went and partied with my crew for another couple of hours before the voices in my head became too much for me to bear. I stood up and walked out of the club without saying a word to anyone and hopped into my Range. I had questions, and I needed answers. There were only two people who could tell me what I wanted to know, so I headed to the condo. I turned my stereo system up as loud as it would go and lit the blunt in the ashtray from earlier. I pressed the start button and spun out of the parking lot. I knew I needed to blow off some smoke before I flipped the fuck out and killed the old man my damn self.

Alizé was the first woman that I could see myself settling down with, and he fucked her. He violated her in the worst possible way, and I don't get what a man that damn old is doing fucking little girls, anyway. There was no way that he didn't know who she was when he did it. She looks so much like her damn daddy. And by all accounts, they were boys back in the day, so he knows what the nigga looks like.

I drove around the city for hours, only stopping to fill up on gas and buy a bottle of liquor. I went to my father's condo prepared to have it out for him once and for all. I knocked on the door a few times, but there was no answer. I got back into my car and rolled another blunt. I was high as fuck, and the liquor was really fucking with my head. I sat there and waited a while longer and went over what I planned to say to his snake ass. The liquor had me feeling myself, and I was ready for whatever.

If he wanted to disown me for choosing love, then so fucking be it. He came to the damn crib a few months back. He met Affinity and didn't even say a single fucking word about her being his daughter or even that she was the daughter of his long-term side bitch. I was going to ask that fucking hoe how the fuck she just left them damn girls to fend for themselves. Everything that my Baby Zé went through is Serena's fault. She shouldn't have left them alone. She should've protected them, but she failed them as a mother and because of her, Alizé lost her childhood and innocence in the worst way.

I pulled my nine out and made sure that bitch was locked and loaded. I wanted answers from them, and I wanted them tonight. I was just finishing my blunt when the sound of a car woke me from the daze that I was in. I looked around and spotted my father's car pulling into the parking lot. I waited for him to get out of the car and tried to calm myself down before I did something stupid. My pops was an OG, so I had to be careful on how I approached him. His ass wouldn't hesitate to pull his strap if he felt like he was losing control of a situation.

"Yo pops, I need to holla at you 'bout some shit," I called out to him.

"Ok, son, are your brother and sister ok?" he replied, as he walked toward me to dap it up, but I bypassed his shit.

"Yeah, both my sisters are ok. No thanks to y'all," I snapped back. I turned my attention to his snake ass bitch. "How could you just leave them? Zé Baby was fourteen! How the fuck did you sleep at night knowing that they were out there in the world alone? Do you fucking know what they have been through 'cuz your hoe ass left them? And what kind of sick motherfucker cuts a nigga's head off in front of his damn kids? Let's not forget, this is the same nigga that admits to fucking his son's chick and his side bitch's daughter. Both of y'all are unfit-ass parents. You knew that was your daughter, and you left her like she was nothing to you. Even when you saw her with Emi, you said nothing." I was fuming. I wanted to blow both these motherfuckers heads off of their shoulders.

"Boy, I am still your father. Watch your fucking mouth when you address me. Now calm the fuck down, and let's go inside and discuss this. You know I don't like my business being discussed in the streets."

As we turned to walk inside the building, I heard someone running up behind us. The three of us turned around just in time to see the hooded figure pulling a strap and aiming it at my dad.

CRACKKKKKK CRACKKKKKK!

The figure fired two shots and ran in the opposite direction.

I pulled my strap and started shooting back. I hit the figure once in the shoulder, but they kept running.

"HELLPPPPPPPPP! SOMEONE HELP US PLEASE!!" Serena started shouting as she rushed to my father's side.

I grabbed my father and tried to stand him up. Throwing my keys to Serena, I told her to open the back doors of my car.

I dragged my father's prone body to the car and struggled to put him on the back seat.

"Apply pressure to the wound!" I barked while I jumped into the front seat and peeled out of the parking lot.

I drove through every red light I went past. I ain't have time to stop for shit. Whoever the fuck did that shit was a good shot, but they were scared. I could see their hand shaking as they pulled the trigger, which is the only reason the second shot missed.

I pulled up right outside the emergency room and hopped out of the car.

"Help me! Quickly, please! My father got shot! I need your help!" Three nurses came running out with a gurney and helped me get my father onto it.

We went inside and gave them his information. I left Serena in the waiting area and phoned my brother.

"Pops got shot. You need to come to the hospital bro. It ain't looking good," I relayed to him.

"What, that nigga ain't my pops. He's your problem." Supreme was slurring, so I knew he had been drinking.

"Nigga just bring your ass on and get the girls. They should both be here. Leave Zé Baby's ass where she at, though. She'll probably come up in here and switch the damn machines off," I told him in all seriousness.

I went outside to smoke another blunt. Sitting in my car, I pulled up the app I had installed, which showed the cameras around the entire crib. I watched as Zé went into her bedroom earlier, then a few hours later, it showed her going downstairs in some little ass shorts and bra. I followed her route as she went into the kitchen to get a bottle of water and then down into the basement where I had installed a gym.

Baby girl was angry as hell. I could tell just by her body movements as she pounded away on the treadmill. I watched her going hard in the gym for over an hour. She then went back into the kitchen, where she sat and spoke with Mrs. A for a while before going back into her room. When she came out of the room forty-five minutes later, she had changed her clothes, and her hair was wet. I watched her go out in the garden, pull out a blunt and face the entire thing. Then I watched as Supreme walked into the garden with a bottle, and the two of them sat there talking until I phoned him.

It fucked my head up that I didn't know who was behind the shooting, but even more so that for a minute, I actually thought my chick did it.

I phoned this pig on my pops payroll and asked him to check the cameras surrounding the building and see at least what car the shooter got into and then to check the hospitals for anyone arriving with a gunshot wound to the shoulder. It was a slim shot though 'cuz I know that most shooters have their own doctor on hand, but I had to do something.

CHAPTER 22

Serena

Sitting in the emergency room waiting to hear how the surgery went and if Chief would be ok was agonizing. I wasn't even allowed to hear the information first. Being that I wasn't family, I had to wait for Knight to tell me what was being said.

I had no idea that he knew my daughters or even that they were in the city until he turned up the other day with Alizé. I know I haven't been the best mother to them, but I would love to see them both. I always knew that Affinity was Chief's daughter, but I never said anything to anyone other than him about it. He refused to accept her as his own because he didn't want Ava to find out the truth.

Knight came back into the waiting area, looking so much like his dad, and sat down near where I was.

"I know you must hate me, Knight, but I didn't leave them. I was admitted to a hospital for six months. I had a breakdown in the street and was taken to the hospital, where they treated me for my mental health issues. I was scared to tell anyone about them out of fear that they would be taken into the system and split up. I know it sounds bad, but I knew

Alizé would cope with Affinity. Please tell me about them. I've missed so much of their lives," I pleaded.

"Shit, you can find out for yourself," he said as he nodded his head in the direction of the entrance, just as a young man walked in with three young women. I turned so I could get a better look at them.

As they walked over to where we were seated, Alizé noticed me and had the meanest scowl on her face as she approached me.

"What the fuck is she doing here, Knight? Y'all got me fucked up today, I swear," she sassed, with her hand on her hip, standing directly between Knight and me.

I stood and walked toward Affinity to hug her. Before I even got near her, Alizé came rushing over to me and punched me in my jaw. I fell to the floor, and she jumped on top of me and was hitting and punching me all over. She was screaming at me about how I had ruined her life the whole time. Eventually, Knight and the other boy pulled her off me.

"Let me go! That bitch deserves everything she gets!" Alizé spat as she was being lifted into the air.

That was the first time I got a good look at the boy who had come in with them. My heart literally stopped for a second when he stared at me.

"Meek?" I mumbled.

"Na bitch you had my daddy killed, remember?" Alizé shot back. "That's my brother. He looks just like daddy though, huh?"

"What the fuck do you mean, your brother? I am the only person to have Meek's kids," I said, feeling hella confused.

"Kid, not kids, remember. Affinity is not his, is she?" Alizé spat back at me.

"Now is not the time for this. I didn't think you were coming, or I would've made her leave," Knight intervened while pulling Alizé onto his lap and holding her tight. Affinity and Empathy sat down next to them, while Meek's son just stood to the side, looking like he didn't want to be here.

"I'm going to get a drink. Does anybody want anything?" I asked.

"No thanks," Knight and Empathy replied while both of my daughters ignored me like I wasn't even there.

I got a cup of coffee and took a seat near the vending machines. I was still in a daze and couldn't believe how such a perfect night had turned into my worst nightmare. After we left the restaurant, I was mad as hell hearing that he'd had sex with my daughter. I was ready to leave his ass until Chief took me to the house that he had just purchased for us. He said it was going to be our fresh start. He was planning to divorce Ava. It was everything I'd been waiting for. I had hoped to hear those words from him for years. Not even four hours after making love to him in front of the fireplace in our brand-new home, I was sitting in the hospital's waiting room, waiting to hear the fate of the man I had spent the last sixteen years of my life loving.

Just seeing my daughters again had me in my feelings. I felt terrible for how I had just left them, but I honestly thought Alizé could handle it until she got in contact with a family member. She was always so grown up for her age. I figured she would just go to Meek's sister or to my brother. I never for a minute thought they would be alone out here in the world. I needed to know what Knight meant when he said that everything that had happened to them was my fault. I could never live with myself if something bad happened in my absence, but I needed that time away to get back to being myself, so I could be the mother they needed.

I was beyond mad to know that Chief had seen Affinity and didn't even tell me. He can play all he wants how he doesn't think she is really his kid but looking at her and Empathy standing next to each other, a blind man could tell that they are related. They look so much alike. They could almost be twins. He should've at least told me that he'd seen her.

I know my daughters deserve an explanation, but I don't know what to tell them. I couldn't admit that I didn't really try to look that hard to find them. The day I got released from the hospital, I went in search of Chief. Eventually, I tracked him down to one of his businesses, and he took me to the condo with him. I stayed there for months without a care in the world. He was spending more time with me and away from that bitch, Ava. After about six months of being free again, I went to my old house so I could see the girls and drop them some money.

When I got to my house, my neighbor told me she hadn't seen them in a few months. I left them a note inside with my telephone number and some money in an envelope. They never phoned me, so I figured they didn't want to see me. Not once did I think they were in any danger, but if I'm honest, I was glad that they didn't want to see me. It just meant I had more time for Chief. I had finally got the man I wanted, and I didn't want anyone ruining our little piece of happiness, and I knew my daughters would do just that.

I snapped out of my thoughts and got another cup of coffee before walking back to join the others. As much as they didn't want me here, I wasn't leaving for shit. They would all just have to get used to my presence in Chief's life. We were together, and no one could tear us apart again. I would make sure of that, just like I made sure Chief found out about Meek and Ava's affair. It just backfired on me when he refused to leave her. I didn't need to worry, though. By all accounts, she lost her shit when he took Meek's head home in a bag that night. For a long time, he blamed me for her leaving, but we had finally got to a place where we were happy. I was not letting Knight or my daughters fuck that shit up for us.

When he found out who tried to kill him, I just knew there would be hell to pay. I couldn't wait to find out who it was.

Just then, the doctor came out. "The family of Chief Carter."

"Here," we said in unison.

"Are you his wife?" he asked me.

"Nah, she's just his side piece. I'm his son, though, so you can tell me what we need to know," Knight added.

"Well, Mr. Carter is an incredibly lucky man. The bullet missed his vital organs, but we can't remove it at this time because it is lodged in his spine. The next twenty-four hours will be touch and go, but we are hopeful that he will make a full recovery. You can go back to see him in just a moment."

"Thank you, doc," Knight said as he shook his hand before he walked away.

I turned back around to take my seat and wait until I was told I could see my man.

"I need to phone my ma, and she's going to want to be here, so you need to kick rocks, lady," Knight's cocky ass said.

"I am going outside, but I will be back regardless of your mother. Your father and I are together, and she knows it. He is getting divorced, and we will be married, so you all need to get used to it. I will not be pushed out. It's me who lives with him and me who he loves." I stood my ground, for once feeling sure of my status in Chief's life.

Walking outside the emergency room doors, I lit up a Newport and walked away from the entrance so I could find a bench to sit on. I don't give a fuck what Ava has to say about my presence. We both knew what it was, and she could go rot in hell with Meek's snake ass for all I cared.

CHAPTER 23

Ava

When we got home from the restaurant, I was angrier than ever with Chief. I can't believe he turned up like that and ruined Knight's birthday dinner. After what he said about being one of the men who violated poor ZéZé, I knew Knight wouldn't be able to cope with hearing that, and it was low, even by Chief's standards. Alizé didn't say a single word in the car on the way home and ran straight up to her room when we got through the door.

I was not about to let this motherfucker think he's won. He doesn't realize that he had just signed his death warrant with the little stunt that he pulled tonight. I went into my bedroom and to my closet. Opening the safe, I took out the brand-new strap I had purchased with a fake ID so it couldn't be traced back to me. I made sure it was loaded and tucked it into the back of my pants. I walked down the stairs and out the door to my car. I know my son has cameras all over the place, so I made sure to look normal as I left. As I pulled up further down the road, I switched cars to a little hooptie I had, especially for occasions such as this, and changed into all black.

With my sneakers on and bandana pulled down over my face, I headed to the condo that my husband shared with his mistress.

I waited outside for what seemed like hours until that fat motherfucker pulled up. When I saw his car pulling into the parking lot, I made sure I was ready. Checking my strap, I quietly got out of the car and crept along the sidewalk behind them. I froze when I heard my son's voice. Knight was walking toward them both with his own strap in hand. He looked drunk and mad as hell. I hid in a doorway until they all turned to walk inside the building. It was too late to back out now, so I ran up behind them. They must've heard me this time, as they all turned around. I let two shots off at him, and he fell to the ground as I ran in the opposite direction, back to my car.

Knight started shooting back, which I wasn't prepared for. He hit me in the shoulder, but I kept running. I got into the car and peeled off. My shoulder was burning like mad. I hit the fingerprint scanner on my phone and scrolled down until I found the number for the only person who I could trust with this, my sister Eva. I pressed call and waited for her to answer.

"Ava, what's wrong? Is everything ok?" she asked, sounding sleepy.

"I need your help. I'll be there in ten minutes."

"What on earth has happened? It's the middle of the damn night. Are you crazy?"

"Eva, I've been shot, and I can't go to the hospital. I need you to never tell anyone about this. I'll explain it all when I get there."

I ended the call and put my foot to the floor. I was bleeding all over my car, so I knew I would have to burn it out when I was finished.

* * *

When I made it to Eva's house, she was waiting at the door for me. When I walked into the dining room, she had already laid out all the things she would need to fix me up and had them on the dining table.

"What have you done now?" she asked.

"I shot Chief."

"You did what now?"

"I know you ain't deaf. I wasn't thinking straight and let my anger get the better of me. I had planned to make it look like he had a heart attack, but I lost my mind tonight and shot at him. The worst thing is that I don't think it killed him. If he ever finds out it was me, he will without a doubt kill me." I started to tell Eva everything as she fixed the hole in my shoulder. It hurt like hell, and at times like this, I wish she still smoked weed.

Finally, she finished stitching up my shoulder. When I was leaving, she hugged me and handed me a small vial.

"All you have to do is empty it into his IV bag, and his heart will stop within an hour or two. It will look like he had a heart attack. I wish you would stop thinking like a ghetto bitch and start using your brain. Just make sure you don't get caught. Come back in a day or two, so I can change the dressing."

"Thank you, Eva," I said, hugging my sister one last time before I left. It was starting to get light outside, so I drove the hooptie over to my brother's junkyard so it could be crushed. From there, I called an Uber to take me back to my car, so I could go home.

When I made it home, I crept upstairs to my bedroom and went to get into a hot bath. My body was aching, and I wanted to lie back, but I had to be careful not to get my dressing wet. Once I washed myself, I climbed into bed.

* * *

When I woke up six hours later, I pulled on my long robe to cover my dressing and made my way downstairs. All the kids were in the kitchen talking, but when I walked in it went quiet and they all turned to look at me.

"Were y'all talking about me?" I asked.

"No, mommy, of course, we weren't. Knight has something he wants to speak to you about." Emi replied.

"Someone shot pops last night," Knight stated.

I spun on my heels and looked at my children. I raised my hand up to my chest, clutching the pearls that weren't even there, and opened my eyes wide with fake shock before I spoke. "Oh my god! Is he ok?"

"He'll be fine. He had to have surgery, but he's expected to make a full recovery. I'm going back to the hospital shortly. Are you going to come with me?" he asked.

"I don't think so, son. I'm glad that he is ok, of course, but it doesn't change things between us. Send him my regards though, won't you? Oh, and have you found out who did it yet? Where was he when it happened?" I asked.

"I don't know yet, but you can bet I've got every nigga on the payroll with their ear to the streets, but no one is talking yet. I'll find out, though. You know how it goes. He was outside the condo. I went there to have it out with him about Zé Baby and ask that bitch how she sleeps at night. Before I got the chance to really find anything out, someone came running up behind us and shot at him. I hit the shooter in the shoulder, so I'm waiting to see if he goes to a hospital."

"I'm sure you'll find out, son. Are you girls going to see your father today?" I asked.

"Yes, both of them are. I know no one agrees but Affi needs to meet him properly. He could've died last night, and she would never have known him. That's not fair to her, and I'll be there the whole time."

I could see that Alizé wanted to say something. Instead,

she kept her composure and remained quiet. Once Knight left with the girls, Supreme told us he was headed to see his girlfriend leaving just me and Zé alone in the house.

"Where did you go last night?" she asked.

"I'll tell you over lunch. Give me an hour to get ready, and we'll go wherever you want," I said with a wink.

It was agony trying to get myself ready properly, but I didn't want to take any painkillers 'cuz I needed to make sure I was on point. I had shit to do, and it had to be done right. It was good to know that they had no leads on who had tried to shoot Chief yet, and I knew they wouldn't find out either. Chief taught me very well, something I'm sure he will come to regret very soon.

* * *

Throwing the keys to Alizé, I told her to drive my Bentley, and she decided we were going for some seafood today. I was opting for some endless shrimp 'cuz I was seriously hungry.

As soon as we ordered our food, Alizé spoke.

"Why did you bring me all the way out here to talk?"

"Knight has cameras in the house. I know you want to know if it was me, and yes, it was. After what he did at Knight's dinner and the awful things he said to you, I couldn't hold off any longer. But I fucked up, and he's not dead. Knight hit me in the shoulder, and so I had to go to my sister's crib and get stitched. She was very fond of your father, but she has always despised Chief. She thinks he ruined my life, which he did. She is the only one who knew of my and Meek's relationship. She even helped us get the house without anyone finding out."

"So, what is our next move? I heard Knight say that they are moving him to a more secure location the moment the doctor says he is ok to travel."

"That's fine. I know where they will be taking him. We have a house on the lake. They'll be headed there. Anytime anything ever happens, that is where he would send the kids and me. Ideally, we need to get him before he gets there, or there will be security covering the whole damn place. This is where you come in. I need you to get Serena away from his room while I put something in his IV bag. You will go and take Knight and the girls some lunch, like the good girlfriend and big sister that you are. You need to act as if you are worried about him. Serena won't be able to resist trying to speak to you, so this time you agree to listen to what she says, keeping Knight there for support. When they are all out of the room, you send me a message letting me know the coast is clear. That's when I go in, dressed as a doctor, and add the stuff to the bag. It'll take around two hours for it to work properly, by which time neither of us will be anywhere near there."

CHAPTER 24

Alizé

I placed an order of food to go and finished eating my food with Ava. When we finished eating, we left the restaurant and made our way to the hospital. I pulled up in the parking lot and got out with the food while Ava went in a different entrance with her bag of clothes to change into.

I found the reception and asked them to point me in the direction of the room of Chief Carter. I waited while she tapped away at her computer for a minute, just to be told that he had already been discharged an hour ago. Turning around, I pulled my phone out of my bag and sent an emergency text to Ava, telling her to go back to the car. Then I phoned Knight and waited for him to answer.

"Hey baby, I brought you and the girls some lunch, but the lady at the receptionist's desk told me that your father has been discharged already," I said when he finally answered.

"Oh yeah, they let the old man leave a few hours ago. I just dropped the girls off at the mall, and I just pulled up outside the condo to check on him. Thank you for thinking of me though. That's why I love your ass."

"Boy, please, that is not the reason that you love me." I laughed.

"Nah, I can think of other reasons too," he replied, laughing.

"Ok, well, just phone me later." I ended the call just as I got back to the car. Ava was already in the front seat clearly dying to know what happened.

I explained to her as we drove back to the house. Just as we pulled out of the parking lot, I saw Knight walking into the hospital hand in hand with a woman. Ava was too busy looking at her phone to notice him, but I saw his ass clear as anything. I was beyond mad at this point and was tempted to stop the car to find out what the fuck was going on.

When we got back to the crib, Ava said she was going to go out to check on her businesses.

I called out, but no one answered. It was the first time I had been in this big old house alone, and I didn't like it one bit. I went upstairs and showered, changing into yoga pants and an oversized sweater. I went back downstairs, and just as I walked into the kitchen, I noticed that the back door was open. I was convinced that it hadn't been like that when I went upstairs an hour ago. Just as I went to close it, I was grabbed from behind and forced down onto the floor. I was fighting to try to get the person off me, but they were a lot stronger than me.

I looked up to see the face of the devil himself. It was Hardcore. His face was scarred real badly, but I would never forget those eyes. The eyes of the man who abused me and made my life miserable for so long.

"Did you miss me, baby?" he said as he pulled me up off the floor.

I was so stunned to see him I couldn't even respond to him. He forced me to sit down in the living room and tied me to a chair. I started freaking out and having flashbacks of the night my daddy was killed. He was tied to the chair, just like I am now. I just knew I would die when Chief was wheeled into the room in a wheelchair.

"You can tell my darling wife that's losing it in her old age. I can't believe she missed the kill shot from such a short distance away. Next time she comes for me, she better kill me 'cuz I'm telling you now, when I see her, I'm at that ass on sight!"

"It wasn't Ava who..."

"Don't fucking lie to me Alizé. You're insulting my intelligence. I know my wife's body very well. I paid for every inch of it to be sculpted to perfection. I came here to give you one last chance to stay away from my son. I am willing to give you one hundred thousand dollars to stay away from him. He will be a very important man, and frankly, he is too good for you. I can't let my son be with a whore who has fucked half the city. Surely you understand. I am giving you twenty-four hours to leave. If you are still in my city after that, I will kill you myself. Untie her, son."

"Pops, you can't be serious. She and that motherfucker Knight tried to kill me, and you expect me to let them live? She emptied my safe, and you're giving her more money?"

"Do as I tell you! Knight is your brother, and you will not harm a single hair on his head! If I have to tell you that again, then you will feel my wrath. You have more money than you know what to do with, so get the fuck over it. Take it as a loss 'cuz Little Miss Alizé is going to leave here unharmed."

Hardcore came up behind me and cut the ropes holding me in place. Chief put a bag down on the floor, and the man pushing him turned him around and led him out of the door. I sat there for a minute, too scared to move. When I finally composed myself, I picked up the bag and walked upstairs to my room. I found my phone and phoned Ava.

"I need you to come home quickly, please!"

She told me she was ten minutes away and would be here soon. It felt like an eternity until I heard a car driving up the gravel driveway. Ava's voice could be heard calling my name, so I went to the bedroom door and called for her to come up.

"He was here, in the house," I said, still shaking.

"Who was sweetie?" she said. Sitting down next to me, she patted my hand.

"Chief was here. With Hardcore, the man who was making me do all that stuff. It's his son, and he knows it was you who shot him. He said he knew your body. You have to be careful."

"What? His son?"

"That's what he said. He gave me one hundred thousand dollars and told me I had twenty-four hours to leave, or he would kill me. What am I going to do?"

"We will have to hide you somewhere far away until he is dead. Then you can come back. We just have to work out what to tell Knight."

"I know what we can say. I wasn't going to mention it to you, but when we left the hospital earlier today, I saw Knight walking hand in hand with a woman, and they were going into the ultrasound department together. I was going to confront him about it when he came home, but you could tell him I saw them, and that's why I left. I know that we have only just got together, but if he had an unresolved situation, I would've rather he told me about it. I don't like being lied to, and if recent events have shown us anything, it's that secrets will always come out. All I know is that after everything he's said to me recently, he better not be still sleeping with this woman."

"Why didn't you say something? We could've confronted him then and there. Never let a man slide, them mother-fuckers start to think they can ice-skate and be slip sliding all over the place. Hell no, son or no son, he is dead ass wrong, and now he will see just how bad it would be to lose you. We about to kill two birds with one stone. Chief will find out that you've left, and Knight will learn a hard lesson about lying."

We came up with a plan for me to leave and go to Myrtle Beach to Ava's sister's condo. I would stay out of the way for a few weeks, then come back and face Knight. I packed a suitcase with a few of my clothes, sunglasses, Kindle, and schoolbooks. I left my phone behind purposely so Knight couldn't contact me but promised that I would ring Ava as soon as possible. I intended to buy a new phone when I got to the airport so we could stay connected. She agreed to explain to Affi that I needed a break and would be home soon. I didn't want to worry her unnecessarily.

I went outside and got into the back seat of the waiting Uber to make my way to the airport. I would have to trust that Ava could pull this off. I was glad to have made it out of there before Knight returned. There is no way he would've let me leave him like that. I didn't want to hear anything he had to say right now, and I didn't know if I would ever be ready to listen to him. I can't believe that Knight has been lying to me this entire time, and I still don't know if he is cheating on me, but since they were walking into the ultrasound department, it's safe to say they've been fucking. He was supposed to be the one man who didn't hurt me. He made me so many promises about how he would protect me and look after me, just to turn around and break my heart. I've never had time away to do whatever I want to, and I'm looking forward to taking some time for me. I had more than enough money never to look back, but I wouldn't leave my sister like that.

* * *

I had never seen anything as beautiful as the condo I was staying in. It is so exquisite with the most breathtaking view I have ever seen. I powered up my new phone and took a picture of the view. I sent a quick message to Ava, telling her I had arrived safely and to phone me when she could talk without Knight or the girls hearing her. I felt bad that I didn't say goodbye to them or my brother, but I couldn't face Knight, and the longer I waited, the more chance there was that he would've caught me.

I got changed into my bikini with a pair of jean shorts. I pulled my hair loose and put my Chanel glasses on my head. I grabbed a bottle of water, and my Kindle and then left to go and sit on the beach for a few hours. I was planning to try and forget everything for the next few weeks. I just wanted to enjoy my vacation and relax. Trying to forget Knight would be hard, but he deserves to sweat for a while. If we are going to have any chance of a relationship, he will have to learn how to treat me. I'm never going to settle for less than I deserve again.

CHAPTER 25

Knight

I hated to lie to Zé Baby when she phoned me earlier, but I couldn't tell her the truth. Today was the day of Nat's first ultrasound, and I finally got her to agree to take a DNA test on her unborn baby to prove if it was my seed that she was carrying or not. I was praying it came back that it wasn't my kid. If it were, then, of course, I would support it, but how the fuck am I gone tell Zé Baby that shit? We're just getting started, and I know this will be too much for her. She will leave me the second she finds out. I know that bitch Nat has got to be lying.

We completed the test, and they told us they would be in touch as soon as the results came back. I dropped Natalia off at home and told her she would hear from me when it was time for the results. She asked me to come in and help her move a few boxes. I didn't want to be an asshole, so I went in and helped her. When I finished moving the boxes out of her spare room, I came back into the living room. She was sitting in the chair, fully naked, and I could hear the gushing noises her pretty pussy was making as she played in it.

She didn't break eye contact with me as she beckoned me

to come closer. I was thinking with the wrong head and started walking over to where she sat. The moment I was in her grasp, she reached up and undone my belt. She pulled my rod free and swallowed it whole. She had that super head game, which made a nigga want to bust in just a couple of minutes. Her sucking game was off the chain, and I spilled my seeds down the back of her throat with a grunt. Seductively, she stood up. It was the first time I really saw the bulge in her stomach. Bending over and holding onto the chair, she spread her legs and looked back over her shoulder at me. Her pussy was glistening from where it was so wet already. It's like it was inviting me in. I plunged my inches into her as deeply as possible without a second thought. It's true what they say about that pregnant pussy. This shit felt so fucking good it should be a crime. As soon as I shot my load over her ass, I was ready to bounce. I pulled my jeans back up and fastened my belt. Nat got up and went to wash, but I didn't wait for her to come back. I just let myself out.

When I got in the car, I instantly felt guilty about Zé Baby. She was a good girl, and she didn't deserve for me to be out here dogging her like that. Regardless of whether this is my kid, I had to make that the last time I got up inside Nat's guts.

* * *

I got home and wanted to get straight into the shower to wash Nat's scent off me before Zé suspected anything. My mom was on my ass the second I walked through the door.

"Boy, you better not tell me I'm about to be somebody's damn grandma? What the fuck is this about you being seen with some woman in the damn hospital?"

"Does Zé know?" I asked.

"It was Alizé who saw you. She's gone, son. I tried to stop

her, but she said she needed some space to think," my mom relayed.

I couldn't fucking believe what was happening. I pulled out my phone to call Zé, but her phone was off.

"Where is she? I need to explain."

"She wouldn't say where she was going. Just that she would be in touch soon. I'm sorry, son, but you fucked up this time," she stated as she kissed my jaw and walked away.

For the rest of the night, I tried ringing Zé repeatedly, but the phone never got turned back on. I found someone I loved and who loved me back, but I fucked it all up for some easy pussy. I was more like my pops than I thought.

* * *

As the days turned into weeks, I felt like Zé wasn't ever going to come back. I was missing my girl like crazy, but my pops had so many business meetings lined up that I hardly had time to think. I'm sure his ass was doing it on purpose. He hated the idea of me being with her, and he was the only one who seemed happy that she was gone.

As I put my suit on to attend yet another meeting, I tried to clear my head, but all I could think about was Zé Baby. I was considering sending a private detective to find her ass so I could bring her home. I just needed to explain and make her understand. The shit with Nat and Liah was before Alizé and I were together. I haven't cheated on her, well, apart from that one night after the ultrasound. I know it was a mistake, but Nat ain't taking it well. She thought we were going to be together after that. She's delusional if she honestly thought I would wife a hoe, but you know how these bitches get.

My brother wasn't really fucking with me too tough. He's pissed that he just found out that she is his sister, and now she's gone. Affi is blanking me altogether, so you know Emi ain't talking to me either. They are both refusing to speak to me until Zé Baby comes home. I won't even get started on my mom. She is big mad at me over the whole thing. She acts like she hasn't spoken to Zé at all, but I know she must've. There is no way that Zé wouldn't check on Affi for this long. It's got me wanting to jack my mom's phone, so I can screen her calls. I just know that she knows more than she is letting on.

Ever since my eighteenth, my pops had been giving me more and more responsibility over the family businesses. The legit businesses were more challenging to learn about than this street shit, but I was all over it, anything which made me money made sense to me. Plus, it was good to be so busy right now. It was the only way that I could get through the hours without pining for Zé.

CHAPTER 26

Alizé

These last few weeks had been hard as hell without Knight. I missed him more than I ever imagined possible. Ava has been finding it hard to get close enough to Chief to kill him, especially now that he knows it was her who shot him. He has literally doubled his security detail since he was discharged from the hospital. She has been studying his schedule and the only time he is alone is when he is in the condo or when he is with Hardcore. Either is good with me 'cuz both Hardcore and Serena needed to go too.

Most days are spent the same. In the morning, I wake up and go to the gym, which is inside the building, for three hours. After I shower and get dressed, I eat and then drive over to the shooting range to practice my aim and build my skills for a few hours. After I finish there, I grab myself a late lunch and sit on the beach reading my Kindle or studying for a while before heading back to the condo. Every night I get into bed missing Knight, remembering the nights when we would just lay in the bed talking and laughing. Of course, I missed the sex. No one has ever made me feel the way he did. I didn't think it was possible to love someone so much but still hate them and be heartbroken over their actions.

The reason behind my regime is simple. I'm going to kill Chief, Serena, and Hardcore. I've had enough of being scared. The first few nights here were the first nights that I had been fully alone in my entire life. No matter what happened, there had always been people around me. It sounds crazy but even having Affinity with me eased the bad feeling that crept over me in the dark.

I had devised a plan to get to them. Each week, they ate at the same restaurant at the same time. I would get a job there and poison Chief's food before it left the kitchen. Ava hooked me up with a guy here who got me a passport, driver's license, and a new social security number. I knew they would be hiring as we were approaching the holiday season. I faked a resume, making it seem like I was perfect for the job. If that failed, I would post up on the roof across the road from Chief's condo and wait for him to come out and pray that my aim was on point.

I've lost a lot of weight, and my body was snatched in all the right places, making my figure look the best it ever has. I've taken my weave out and been rocking my natural hair. I've got a lace front curly red wig, and some colored contact lenses to help disguise myself when I go back. I look so different that even I don't recognize myself. The plan was to go back to the city over the weekend and stay in a hotel until I made it happen. I just had to avoid Knight or anyone I knew until I was ready for them to do so.

* * *

Walking out of O'Hare International Airport, I was happy to be back in the place that I now considered home. I caught a taxi to the Lakeshore Hotel. I had already booked a room for two weeks. I hoped that by the time those two weeks were up that I could go home to be with Knight. My interview for the position at Cite was tomorrow morning, and I had to make sure I got the job. Ava said she would teach me what I needed to know. I couldn't wait to see her later. In the brief time we'd known each other, we've become good friends. I know I would've loved her as a stepmom, and it's sad that the love she shared with my daddy had to end before either of them was ready.

Ava told me that the day Knight was at the hospital, he was with a woman who claimed that she was pregnant with his child. Their relationship was before we got together, so I couldn't be too mad other than the fact that it should've been me about the girl and the baby. I wanted to build a life with this man, and that life included lots of babies, but I never thought that there would be children made outside our relationship. If it is his kid, I will love it because it's his, but I'm not even going to front and act like I don't hope it's not. Either way, it is not the child's fault, so I would never project my feelings onto them. It only dawned on me this morning that my period was late. Unlike last time, I'm not scared. If I am pregnant, then there is no doubt in my mind that I will have this baby. This baby was created out of love, pure all-consuming love.

Lately, I've had so much time on my hands that I've been thinking deeply about my life and the direction I am going. It's time I thought about my future and what career I want to have. I knew I would be with Knight again. I had no doubt in my mind that we were meant to be together, but I didn't want to be one of those women who stayed at home, catering to her man twenty-four hours a day. Now, I will cater to my man, of course, but I need to have a career as well.

I had plans to be an interior designer, but I also want to do some kind of volunteer work with vulnerable teens, kids who are just like I used to be, good kids who just got a shit hand in life. If I could save girls from going down the same path that I had to, it would be worth it.

I enjoyed my time with Ava. It felt so good just to have a conversation with someone. The whole time I was away, I barely interacted with anyone. She filled me in on everything that's been happening at home. She told me that neither Affi nor Emi were speaking to Knight. You know that was hurting him. He loved his little sisters, so for neither of them to be speaking to him was fucking him up for sure. I can bet he's buying them all sorts of gifts to win them round.

I was excited as hell for my interview. I just wanted to get this over with. I was scared that if I left Knight for too long, he would move on without me, so it was imperative that I got myself back home with my family.

The Next Morning

"Well, Miss Jackson, you seem to be qualified enough and you certainly fit the image we are looking for. You can come in for a trial shift this evening, and if you do well, you will be offered the position," the posh white man told me as he licked his lips while looking me over.

"Thank you, sir. I won't let you down," I replied happily.

I practically skipped out of there. Once in the elevator, I pulled out my phone to send Ava a message letting her know I had a trial run for the position that evening.

On my way back to the hotel, I spotted Hardcore. Luckily, he didn't recognize me being that I had my wig on and some oversized Chanel glasses covering my face. I decided to follow him. For him to be the son of one of the most powerful men in the city, he was dumb as fuck. Not once did he check his surroundings. Ava had told me that his mother was a white woman who had gotten hooked on crack after

Chief broke off their relationship. Her name was Tracey. Sadly, she overdosed a few years back. Chief's father had banned them from being together, saying she wasn't good enough for him and that they were too young. They were only fourteen when he was born. When I was there with him, Hardcore told me that his mother had left him when he was young, and he had grown up being in and out of care homes until an older couple took him in. It turns out it was Chief's brother and sister-in-law. It clearly fucked him up, but he must be mad that Chief never once claimed him or cared for him. Instead, paying for him to be cared for by his uncle and aunt. Ava filled me in on everything, although until the day they came to the house, she didn't even realize that they were in contact.

Later that evening, as I went back for my trial shift at Cite, I knew I had to impress the manager, but as he was a bit of an old pervert, I made sure to wear a tight shirt and skirt. If there is one thing that I know how to do it is to make a man think I want them. Hardcore used to make us pretend as if the client were special, so they believed we were interested in them, so I knew how to flatter a man and batt my eyelashes a few times to make them putty in my hand, and this man would be no different.

As the restaurant was so busy, the night flew by. I got the hang of it pretty quickly and easily impressed the old man. He offered me the position and quietly told me I was that good and that he would ensure I was quickly waiting on the VIP tables. Little did he know, I was only planning to be there two more nights until Chief and Serena's usual Friday night date. Ava had gotten a hold of something which I just had to put into the food, and it would make his heart stop. It was a kind of poison, but it was odorless and tasteless, so hopefully, he wouldn't detect it.

* * *

By Friday night, I was so nervous that I thought I was going to piss on myself. I made sure that my wig was on point and my face was beat to perfection. Looking in the mirror, I knew that they wouldn't recognize me. You knew the money had gone to my mother's head, as neither of them even looked up from the menu or even made eye contact with me. It was like I was invisible to them. Once the food was ready and put on the line for me to take out, I had to hurry. I removed the lid from the poison and poured the entire contents of the vial all over Chief's main course. Taking the food to the table, my hands were shaking. I kept telling myself to hold it together just a bit longer. Just as before, neither of these ignorant motherfuckers even looked at me.

I went back to my post and watched as his fat ass devoured the whole meal. I felt butterflies in my stomach as he ate. I kept waiting for him to keel over right there, but I knew it would take an hour or two before it really took effect. It was so difficult trying to keep my composure as they sat and made small talk over dessert. When they ordered the bill and left, still without even glancing in my direction, I knew my plan had gone perfectly.

The second my shift ended, I rushed back to the hotel and phoned Ava.

"I did it. I actually did it!" I said excitedly.

"Well done, baby. Now we just have to wait. I'm parked outside the restaurant in a rental car, so I saw you leave. I've put a tracking device on his car, so I will come to the hotel now. We can track the car using the app on my phone.

Ending the call, I waited for Ava. I ordered a bottle of

champagne from room service, ready to celebrate. After tonight, I would be free to go home and claim my man.

* * *

We watched as the marker on the app, which represented Chief's car, drove back to the condo. We finished up our drinks, then returned to the rental car and drove over to his condo. Just as we arrived, there were flashing red lights and two paramedics wheeling someone out on a gurney. We followed behind them as they made their way to the hospital. We parked up and spectated as the medical team got out of the ambulance looking sad, and Serena dropped to the floor in floods of tears, crying. They were in no rush to get Chief inside, which told us he was already dead before they arrived at the hospital.

Smiling, Ava dropped me back off at the hotel and told me she would phone me and let me know when she heard something. I was too excited to sleep, so I packed up all my stuff and got ready to go home tomorrow. Knight will need me, and when he finds out about his dad being dead, I'm going to go home and be the supportive girlfriend. I will address the situation with the pregnant woman, but first and foremost, I have to be there for my man in his time of need. I'm not sorry that Chief is dead. I'm just sorry I had to hurt Knight and Empathy in the process. Still, at least now I know that Knight and I can have a chance at a happy future without the cloud of his dad's actions hanging over us. I finally got to avenge my dad's murder, which feels pretty good to me.

CHAPTER 27

Ava

I hated being the reason my kids were hurting, but that nigga had it coming for a long time. After leaving ZéZé at the hotel, I went home. My kids were all home by the time I made it there, and Knight's nosy ass wanted to know where I had been. After lying to him about having dinner with my sister, I sat and chatted with him for a while. It was going on midnight when his phone started ringing. Excusing himself, he went to take the call outside. Two minutes later, he came walking back into the house, looking like he was lost.

"What's wrong, son?" I asked as I got up to hug him.

"It's pops," he said as a tear rolled down his face. "He's dead."

"Oh my god, baby. What happened?"

"That was Serena. She said they came back from dinner, and he wasn't feeling well. The next thing she knew, he fell to the floor, shaking. She phoned for an ambulance, and when the paramedics got there, they tried to revive him, but he was pronounced dead before they even arrived at the hospital. Uncle Major is there now. He's called an emergency meeting for the entire crew. I have to go. Will you tell the girls for me, please? Neither of them is fucking me right now. I'll phone Reme on the way to the hospital." With that, he walked out the door.

As soon as his car spun out of the driveway, I picked up my phone and phoned Zé.

"It worked. He's gone. Knight has been called to an emergency meeting with his uncle. He isn't aware of it yet, but I watched the same thing happen when my father-in-law died. Knight is about to be put in charge of the family businesses. He's going to be a boss now, and he'll need a boss bitch by his side, so you need to put your big girl panties on and step up for your man. This is your time to shine as the queen, and it's time that you came and reclaimed your rightful place next to your man. Wait a couple of hours and come home, baby girl."

"We're not done just yet. I won't be happy until Serena and Hardcore are both gone, too. Hardcore will not be happy that Knight is being crowned king, although he is the oldest. I feel like he will try to take Knight down if we don't stop him."

"Ok, one down, two to go. It will be much easier now, and neither of them will be protected without Chief. His family will never accept Serena, the side bitch or the illegitimate son that should've never been born," I reassured her.

Alizé was right, though. We would have to do something about the bastard child first. Then I would have my fun watching Serena fall apart again. They say revenge is sweet, but you have no idea how sweet it really is.

I made my way upstairs to tell the girls that their daddy was dead. It wouldn't be an easy conversation, but they would be better off without him in the long run. I just had to remember to try and look sad when I broke the news.

Empathy was understandably more hurt by the news of Chief's passing than Affinity was. They sat on the bed, cuddled up, seemingly lost in their own thoughts. I left them, letting them know I was there for them if they wanted to talk.

It was almost daylight by the time I got into my bed, but I couldn't sleep. The adrenaline was pulsing through my veins. I couldn't believe that we'd managed to actually pull it off and that asshole Chief was finally burning in hell. Looking over at the picture of Meek and me on my nightstand, I smiled.

"We finally did it, baby. You can rest in peace now."

* * *

A couple of hours later, I heard the door open and shoes clicking across the foyer. Seconds later, Alizé came walking up the stairs with her suitcase. She looks like a completely different woman than the young girl I met all those months ago. She's got a new sense of confidence that I love about her. With a bit of training, she will be a force to be reckoned with. She's ready to be the down ass bitch my son needs. Knight had better learn quickly that she was not the same girl she once was and let's just hope he acts right this time because I would hate to see him lose her over something stupid. I can't wait to see the new and improved Alizé and watch her shine.

CHAPTER 28

Knight

I got to the hospital to see my pops' body. It fucked me up to see him lying there still and lifeless. My uncle came walking into the room, looking like a younger version of my pops. We stood for a minute, paying our respects before he turned to me and let me know he had come to take me to the meeting.

Nothing could've prepared me for the sight in front of my eyes. There were heads of all the families, and they were there to watch me take my place in line as the head of the Carter family. It felt weird as hell that everyone was celebrating me when I should be mourning the loss of my pops, but real g's don't die. He'll live on in our memories forever.

* * *

When I got home, I was absolutely exhausted. I just wanted to lay up under my Zé Baby, but the chance would be slim. She's been gone almost a month, and I've not heard anything from her. It was already going into the afternoon when I pulled up outside the crib. I just sat deep in thoughts as I smoked the rest of my blunt before I headed inside to sleep for a few hours.

When I walked into my bedroom, I was on autopilot. I walked straight into the bathroom. I ripped off my clothes and showered quickly. When I walked back into my room, my heart jumped out of my chest looking at Zé Baby sleeping in my bed. I hadn't noticed her when I first walked in. Slowly I got in behind her and pulled her close to my chest. No words were needed as I felt her snuggle into my body. A light snore escaped her mouth, but she never woke up. I fell to sleep, holding her tight like I was scared to let her go in case I lost her again.

When I woke up hours later, she wasn't there. I jumped out of bed, threw on some shorts, and ran down the stairs, almost tripping and falling flat on my face. When I got into the kitchen, I saw her cooking with my mom and Mrs. A, and the relief washed over me.

"Hey," she quietly greeted as she turned and noticed me watching her.

"I'm so sorry, baby. I missed you so much." I grabbed her and picked her up. Wrapping her legs around me, I nestled into her neck and held her tightly. "I can explain everything. please don't leave me like that again."

"Your mom phoned me last night and told me the news about your dad. I'm sorry that you're going through this, baby. I won't pretend I like him, but I love you, so I'm here. I'm home to stay, but you're right. You do have some explaining to do later," she said as she kissed me deeply.

If there it's one thing I learned, it's that life is too short. I wanted to be with Alizé forever, so I knew what I had to do. I was putting a ring on her ass and holding her down for life. I carried her back up the stairs and straight into my bedroom, where I made love to her for hours. We spent the rest of the night in the bedroom, making up for the lost time.

* * *

When I woke up the following morning, I was a man with a plan in mind, and I wanted to do it all today, but first, I owed my baby an explanation. So, we sat down, and I explained to her about Nat. I found out a couple of days ago that she had moved out of her crib and disappeared. I had people looking for her, but no one knew where she was. After waiting over three weeks, I finally got the DNA test results, and it turns out that the baby she's carrying isn't mine. I know that's why her ass went ghost on me. She knew I would be angry about her lying to me, especially considering her lies caused me to lose my girl.

I wasn't the only one who had been hiding some news, though. I couldn't believe it when Zé Baby told me she was pregnant. This time, hearing those words made me happy as hell. Zé was the only woman I could see myself raising kids with. I couldn't wait to break this news to the family.

I took Zé out for lunch and then dropped her off to get her hair done. While she was getting her inches laid in the salon, I went to the jewelry store to get her a ring. I sent a group text to the whole family and told them I wanted us to have a family dinner as I had some news that I wished to share with them.

I met up with my uncle to discuss getting my pops' funeral sorted out, but the police weren't trying to release his body just yet, so we had to keep waiting. The arrangements were in place, and the second we got his body back, he would have a funeral fit for a boss. I'd chosen a black casket with eighteen-carat gold accents and a silk lining that was woven with real gold. I had a hundred white doves which were being released at the burial. His final resting place would be in the Carter mausoleum, alongside my grandparents, aunt, and two cousins. We were having the service at the same church where my parents and grandparents married, and the casket would be carried by myself, Supreme, my two uncles, and two of my father's lieutenants. The only thing left to do was keep my mom and Serena away from each other during the services. There will be too many important people there for them to make a show of themselves by fighting over a dead man. I just pray that they both have some sense and act right, even if it is just for a few hours.

Later that night, while the whole family was sitting around the table, I looked around, from each of my siblings to my mom, Mrs. A, and my beautiful Zé Baby. For the first time ever, I realized just how lucky I really was. My family was amazing, and I couldn't wait to add another person to the mix. Now that Zé was back, my sisters loved me again, and my brother looked happy for a change. When I tell you, none of them were fucking with me while Zé was gone. I mean it. They wouldn't even look in my direction, let alone speak to me.

"We've got some news that we want to share with y'all," I said as they all turned to look at me. "Baby, do you want to tell them?" I asked.

"So, while I was away, I found out that I'm pregnant. We're having a baby in seven months."

My mom almost choked on her Bellini. "You're what now?" she said, with her eyebrows raised high, and we all laughed. "I'm too damn young to be anyone's grandma. Are y'all trying to kill me? Oh lord, I'm about to be a Glam ma, ain't no one calling me no grandma."

Everyone congratulated us, and we enjoyed the rest of the

meal. I was starting to get nervous as hell. My palms were sweating, and I had to wipe my brow. It was now or never.

"There is something else," I noted as I pushed my chair out so I could stand.

"Oh Lord, take the wheel. I'm still getting over the shock of the baby. What the hell you want to say now, boy?" My mom's dramatic ass said while clutching the pearls which we knew weren't around her neck.

I stood up and moved my chair, then dropped to one knee as I pulled the ring box from my jacket pocket.

"Baby, these last few weeks without you have been hell. I know I fucked up, but I would never do anything to hurt you intentionally. I want to love you and be with you every single day of my life. You make me want to be a better man, and now you are giving me the best thing in the world, our own family. I don't want my seed coming into this world without you rocking my last name. Will you marry me, baby?"

The tears streamed down Alizé's face, and she nodded her head yes. "Yes, baby, I'll marry you."

I slid the ring onto her finger and stood up to kiss my fiancée. My family started clapping, and we all toasted the engagement.

* * *

Over the next few weeks, Zé, the girls, and my mom organized the wedding, while my uncle and I had to arrange a funeral. Them people finally released my pops' body. The funeral would be first, out of respect for my pops, although I know he would be turning in his grave at the thought of me marrying Zé Baby. You know how the saying goes. You can't help who you love. Something he proved to us all when he got with that bitch Serena. Part of me so desperately wanted to put her out on her ass, but after the reading of the will, I felt a little bad for her. She put a lot of time into that man and tolerated a lot from him, so it must've hurt her to be left with nothing. Although, he did apparently have an appointment to amend his will, which he never made it to. I told her she could keep the condo and I would find a job for her in one of the businesses, but in return, I would expect her to leave Zé alone and not to contact her.

The day of the funeral came, and I knew I would be expected to act like a boss, which meant I would have to keep my game face on and not show any weakness. I knew that all eyes would be on me as the new head of the family, and if anyone thought we were weak, they were bound to try something stupid. There would be a fight for power and territory. Neither of which I was prepared to lose, so I knew I had to stay strong. Zé agreed to come with me for support. I know she didn't care for my pops, and I don't blame her. I'm just happy as hell that she'll be here to hold my hand through all of this.

As we stepped into the church, it was already packed with family, friends, and business associates. There was a heavy police presence outside. With that many known criminals and gang members in the building, they feared something would pop off. Everyone turned around to look at us as we walked down the aisle to the front pew so we could take our seats. My mom and Serena locked eyes, and I half expected my mom to tell her to move, but she didn't. Instead, she took the seat next to her, followed by Zé, Affi, Emi, Reme, and me. Serena looked scared as hell that my mom was so close to her, but I know my mom, and she won't do anything in front of these people. She would always appear to have the upper hand in a situation, even if she were losing all control. It was a front that she put on in public, and being with my father, it was something she'd managed to perfect.

It warmed my heart to see just how many people had come out to honor my father. As I turned around, I spotted a face in the back of the crowd. He looked really familiar, but his face was covered in burns. When I looked again, he had gone. The man's face was stuck in my head. All day I was trying to place him, but I couldn't think where I knew him from.

* * *

As the weeks went by, the wedding got closer. Alizé and my mom were having so much fun planning it. What was originally going to be a small affair soon turned into a lavished celebration. As I had recently inherited my father's fortune, money was no object. What my baby wants, she gets.

The last thing I needed was Liah turning up and claiming that her baby was mine. Just when I thought I was rid of Nat's lying ass, this bitch turns up with the same bullshit and a baby in her arms. She came to me telling me her man kicked her out of the house with the baby because he knew it wasn't his child. She claims they weren't even sleeping together at the time, but I don't believe a word any of these hoes say. I felt sorry for her, though, and I couldn't see her out on the streets with a baby, so I've been hiding her out in a hotel downtown until I could get the DNA test done. I just got Zé back, and now I've got to explain to her that yet again, another bitch is claiming she's got my kid. She will go crazy when she finds this out, especially being pregnant. Her hormones are all over the place already. Call me selfish all you want, but I have every intention of not letting Alizé find out that shit until after we're married. There ain't no way in hell I'm losing baby girl again.

I never expected these kinds of problems from Liah. I know she had a man at home, so I don't know why she thinks

I would take her word for it. What kind of nigga ain't notice that their chick is out fucking around all the damn time? Liah was a party girl, so I was shocked when I found out that she had kids.

I can't think of all that shit now. Tonight is the night of my bachelor party, and you know the whole crew came out to celebrate with ya boy on his last night of freedom. As I sat drinking the bottle of Rémy straight out the bottle, I thought back over the last few months, and I couldn't believe how much my life had changed. If you'd told me a year ago that I would be about to get married and have a baby, I would've thought you were crazy. It just goes to show that you don't know what's around the corner. I thought of my pops, and I knew that despite the things he's done over the years, his absence would have an enormous impact on not only my life but those of my sisters too. I had some pretty big shoes to fill, but I was confident I had it in me to deal with whatever lies ahead and remain true to the game.

My crew was all around me, watching the baddest strippers the city had to offer, but even with all that ass in my face, all I could think about was Zé Baby. I wish I could just go home and get in the bed with her tonight, but I've been put out of the house with strict orders that I am not to come back before the wedding.

CHAPTER 29

Alizé

It's the morning of my wedding, and I have never felt so nervous in my life. Supreme was giving me away, and it felt like I had my dad with me. He was so much like him that it really made me happy to know that, in some small way, my father lived on through us both.

The whole glam squad arrived early this morning and spent the last four hours helping us get ready for the big day. When I saw the dresses again this morning, they looked even better than I remembered. It's amazing that we found the perfect dresses in such a short space of time. Affinity and Empathy were bridesmaids wearing turquoise dresses in unique styles to complement their different body shapes. My dress was like something you've only ever seen on the glossy pages of *OK!* magazine. It was a thirty-five-thousand-dollar, custom-made Vera Wang princess-style dress with a huge train. Looking in the mirror when I was fully dressed, I couldn't believe just how beautiful I looked.

I was speechless. My eyes started to water, and I tried to blink away the tears that threatened to fall. After all that I have been through, just to be standing here in my big dress, knowing I am marrying the man of my dreams, is more than I ever thought possible. I honestly considered taking my life and ending my misery at one stage, but I could never leave my sister. Looking back, those dark days seem so far behind me that it's like a whole lifetime ago.

We hadn't been able to follow through with the plan to kill Hardcore or Serena yet, but I'm confident we will get them sooner rather than later. I'm not going to be scared anymore. I've already got through what should've killed me, so I can handle them both. Ava has been teaching me how to be the wife of a boss. I stay ready, and my aim is on point, so the next time they approach me on some bullshit, they can feel my heat. I said goodbye to Alizé, the victim, and hello to Zé Baby, the boss bitch. That weak shit is dead. The new me isn't tolerating bullshit from anyone anymore.

As the limo arrived to take us to the church, we walked outside together to get in the car. I got downstairs, and the photographer was snapping away pictures for my wedding album. I noticed a woman standing to the side, holding a baby. I thought it was strange as I'd never seen her before, so I wondered why she was at my wedding. Once the pictures were finished, we turned to climb inside the car. The woman walked toward me like she wanted to speak to me, but Supreme stood directly in front of me like he was shielding my body. He was so overprotective, and I've got to admit that I loved it. He pushed me into the car, getting in behind me. He closed the door, and the driver pulled off, leaving the woman standing there.

When I started my walk down the aisle, my legs felt so weak that I thought I would fall. Luckily, my brother was there to hold me up. I was in awe at how beautifully Ava and the girls had decorated the church. The vast array of flowers that adorned the ends of each row of seats looked and smelled amazing. As Knight turned around to look at me, my heart skipped a beat. He looked so handsome in his black Tom Ford tux, with his home boys standing in a line next to him, all wearing matching suits. They were so damn extra, but I got to admit they all looked good as hell. Looking at them, you would never know that they were all street niggas and thugs.

As we said our vows, there wasn't a dry eye in the entire church. Everyone clapped as we jumped the broom, and when we got outside, people were throwing confetti all over us. It was the best day of my whole life, and I never wanted it to end.

* * *

When I walked into the banquet hall where the reception was being held, I couldn't believe my eyes. It looked like something out of a fairy tale, and there were pictures of us projected onto a huge ass screen, so everyone could see them. Our vision looked even more beautiful once we brought it to life.

Everyone was having a great time. We had a huge seven-course meal prepared by a well-known celebrity chef and music from some of the hottest names in the business. The entire day looked like the kind of wedding you would see in a magazine.

I couldn't see Knight anywhere, so I went into the hall to see if he were with the guys shooting dice. I asked one of his boys if he had seen him, and he said he thought he was outside. So, walking outside, I spotted him. He was deep in conversation with the woman outside the house earlier today.

"Liah, what the fuck are you doing here? I told you to stay out of the way today. We will take the test, but not fucking today! I won't let you fuck this up for me. You and Nat were both a fucking mistake. if I could take it back, I wouldn't have fucked with either of you."

"She is your baby Knight. Just look at her!" she cried.

They were both so engrossed in their conversation that

neither of them noticed me until I was right behind him, but by then, it was too late. I'd heard enough to know that I wanted to get the fuck out of there.

I turned on my heels and walked back into the building to get my belongings, with Knight following closely behind me. I walked straight over to the table where we were sitting and asked Ava to pass me the key to the suite.

"What is wrong, baby girl? You can't leave. It's your big day," she spoke.

"There is a woman outside with my husband. Did you know he has a baby daughter?" I asked her.

"No, the test came back saying it wasn't his child," she tried to pacify me.

"NO! It's a different woman, Ava! I need to leave. I can't be here. He promised he wouldn't hurt me, but he knew about her. I heard him saying that he warned her not to come today. I can't do this. Every time I get close to Knight, I get hurt. It's not just me I have to consider. I am his wife. It should only be me having his child, not some random bitch! After everything I've been through, this is too much."

Knight finally reached me after making his way through the crowd of people passing him envelopes and greeting him.

"Baby, just let me explain. Please, Alizé, just speak to me."

"I don't want to hear it, Kni..." before I could finish my sentence, the entire hall went quiet, and the music stopped.

I turned around to see the place being stormed by at least ten FBI agents with guns drawn. They made a clear path for two plain-clothes detectives who made their way toward where we were standing.

"Alizé Washington, or is it, Carter, now? We have a warrant for your arrest in the murder of Chief Carter. You have the right to remain silent. Anything you say can and will be used against you in a court of law. You have the right to an attorney. If you cannot afford an attorney, one will be appointed to you. Cuff her and let's go. If anyone tries anything stupid, I will have you in jail within an hour. Let's go."

The next thing I knew I was being led away from my wedding in handcuffs with a detective on either side of me under the glare of my husband's entire crew, the same crew who worked for my late father-in-law. The look of contempt in their eyes told me that given the chance, most of them would kill me before I got outside if they thought they could get away with it. Some of Chicago's top hittas were in the building, and had I not been surrounded by so many officers of the law, I wouldn't have made it out of the building alive. My sister was crying, and Ava was demanding answers that nobody was giving.

Knight just stared at me, not saying a word. In this moment, my perfect existence was shattered right before my eyes, and there wasn't a thing I could do to stop it. The man I trusted more than anyone in the world turned out to be a fraud, but who was I kidding? So was I. I killed his dad and held him while he grieved the loss. I just knew everything was too perfect. Who was I kidding? People like me don't get the happily ever after we're looking for.

As I sat in the back of the police car waiting to be taken to jail, the look on Knight's face told me he would never forgive me for this...

Want to be a part of the Grand Penz Family?

To submit your manuscript to Grand Penz Publications, please send the first three chapters and synopsis to grandpenzpublications@gmail.com